Suitable Husband

Denisthorn Hall Series
Book Two

Rosanne Dingli

Yellow Teapot Books Australia

Yellow Teapot Books Australia

Historical Fiction

ISBN: 9798323441815

Cover picture *Mrs Brassey*
by Francis Grant, 1853
Author picture by Mark Flowers
Designed and typeset in Constantia by
Ding! Author Services

Also by Rosanne Dingli

Death in Malta
Camera Obscura
According to Luke
The Hidden Auditorium
The Frozen Sea
The Cartographer of Venice
The White Lady of Marsaxlokk
How to Disappear
A Funeral in Fiesole
Petals & Pages
A Place in Society

For more about this author visit
rosannedingli.com

This volume was delayed by a series of interruptions that in themselves would have made a reasonable novel. Summoning motivation and energy to complete a work can be challenging even when things are going well. Nothing would have happened without the help of my exceptional BETA readers, among whom Petronella Catharina proved to be a champion. The whole work benefited from precise scrutiny by Teena Raffa-Mulligan. And new spectacles proved valuable, of course.

A SUITABLE HUSBAND

DENISTHORN HALL
BOOK TWO

CHAPTER ONE

In which the Croukerne sisters have a quarrel
and
the countess shows signs of distress

A housemaid raised a finger to her lips. Another fell silent. Loud words could be heard along the gallery, which overlooked the grand hall, and whose valuable Turkish carpets hushed footsteps. Even at that early time of morning, when only servants had the run of the house, loud words were being shouted in a most unladylike manner. The owners of the strident voices did not seem to care there was a servant on the stairs, carrying a bowl of flowers to the gallery, or that another was tending the twin fires on either side of the hall.

A footman left the drawing room through its tall double doors. It was a good thing neither Mrs Beste, the housekeeper, nor Mr Herring, the butler, were anywhere in the vicinity, because the servants, who could not see each other at first, but quickly gathered at the bottom of the stairs, looked meaningfully—but silently—at each other.

What was the commotion about?

The voices were female, young, and vociferous. Some of the words they said seemed unintelligible, others rather clear. Ladies Athena and Geraldine were having a disagreement in the corridor outside their rooms, at that ungodly hour of the morning.

As one of the servants raised finger to lips once more, they drew together and looked upward. They could see nothing but the underside of the elaborate carved gallery, and perhaps the framed tops of all the portraits hanging above, but their eyes travelled upward regardless, and then back at each other. One smiled, another pursed her lips onto a silent 'Oooh!', a third shrugged, and they remained standing in silence, straining to listen.

'How dare you say that, Athena?'

'I dare—because I'm still older than you are. I always will be. And just because you are engaged to be married to Angus Crownrigg, it doesn't mean you've added anything in numbers of years, or level of privilege, or presumption of honour or position!' It was a long sentence for the older daughter, who usually exclaimed little else but monosyllables. Since her sister's engagement, however, it was as if her tongue was cut loose.

'Level of privilege?'

'You have taken a different attitude, even with the servants. And you expect to have Fairley attend to you alone. How you imagine that you can have our lady's maid all to yourself, I do not know.' Athena huffed. 'You'll expect to have my place at table next, and pretend to all the world that you are the older daughter, the first-born, rather than me.'

'I pretend no such thing!'

'There is no need to shout. You protest to all who will listen, and flounce around expecting Mama to respond to all your demands and wishes. It's as though all the world is watching and waiting. It's weeks until your wedding, and yet the house is in complete disarray and confusion.'

Geraldine could be heard to stamp her foot on the exquisite Turkish carpet in the gallery.

A servant below raised a hand to conceal a smile.

Another stamp was heard. Lady Geraldine's feet beat a tattoo on the floor. 'You keep saying *all the world*. What do you mean by that? We're cloistered here at Denisthorn, we hardly ever see a new face. What world? All we see are Papa, Mama, and the servants!'

'Oh, Geraldine. You'll presently be off to Aunt Margery's. Stop. Stop, I say. Calm yourself. Come into your room and show me your trousseau once more. Show me your new clothes, won't you?'

'Fairley is doing my packing!'

'What—at this ridiculous hour?'

'It needs to be done.'

'Oh, pray stop. And then we might ...' A door was heard to slam behind them, leaving a wake of silence. Leaving the servants to wonder whether Lady Athena succeeded in appeasing young and excited Geraldine, who, after weeks of wondering whether she had done the right thing in accepting Angus Crownrigg, now charged about the entire house in a flurry of excitement about her forthcoming nuptials.

The atmosphere was altogether calmer later on, in Lady Croukerne's day sitting room, even if a tinge of excitement, and the exhilaration brought about by preparation for an extraordinary event, filled the air. Ensconced with her ladyship were Mrs Beste, with her pencil and notebook, and Cook, which was what everyone called Mrs Jones, a small thin woman with a permanent crease between her eyebrows. She had an extraordinarily neat and fastidious appearance.

'You'll not be surprised to hear you have quite a name in the district, Mrs Jones.'

'I am flattered I'm sure, your ladyship, but I cannot see how that could possibly be.'

'It is. Perhaps it is the fact you have won the village pork pie competition three years running. Your skills at pastry-making and cake-baking are well known in these parts. And that is the reason I shall entrust to you, together with other culinary duties, the onerous task of making the bride cake.'

A rare smile spread slowly on Cook's face. 'Oh! My lady!' Her hands fluttered to her throat, but she quickly brought them back to fall stiffly by her sides. 'And would your ladyship desire a high cake, a wide square cake, or—as I have seen in a recent magazine—a *round* cake with many layers? Iced, of course. But will it be pound cake, or fruit cake?'

Lady Croukerne frowned, smiled, and frowned again. 'A wide cake, I should imagine. Wide *and* round! A rich fruit cake, iced in white over a generous layer of the best marzipan, decorated sparingly. There will not be a groom cake, since I feel ... Yes, Mrs Beste?'

'Might I point out that the fashion for groom cakes has gone extinct, my lady.' Mrs Beste looked up from her book. 'One can have two bride cakes, perhaps, or just the one wide cake as a centrepiece, surrounded by platters of other sweetmeats.' She looked at Cook. 'Mrs Jones, how do you feel about continental *petits fours*?'

Real excitement accompanied those words.

'Yes, yes. Petits fours!' The countess liked the idea.

'There are three types of petits fours, your ladyship, and luckily, since we have more than two ovens in the kitchens, we could possibly ...'

'Three kinds, Cook!' The countess was rather intrigued.

'Sugar-glazed, savoury, and dry pastries. All small, all dainty.'

'Very elegant.'

'Oh yes! Very fashionable, too. They are time-consuming, and the quantities of ingredients call for adequate supply.' She raised a discreet eyebrow.

'Oh, I meant to say, Cook, please ensure there are another two or three girls to help in the kitchen. I'm sure some hard workers can be found in the village.' The countess nodded at Mrs Beste. 'And you are definitely to have ample quantities of all the ingredients called for in the recipes, Mrs Jones. *Of course.*'

So it was decided. There would be a big formal dinner, with many guests, and the dessert course would be replaced by a cake course.

'I suppose I must speak to his lordship about music.'

Both women looked at the countess, knowing she still grieved deeply for her young son, and was emotionally and in manner, if not in dress, still in mourning.

'Music? Music ... like we used to hear emitting from a small music box. I see Frederic, you know. I see him through that window, running along with his hoop and stick.'

The servants looked at each other without a word. The silence was as eloquent as if one of them had asked the countess whether she was quite all right.

'I see him on the stairs. And in the small library.'

'Your ladyship.'

Edwina, Lady Croukerne, wife of the fifth Earl of Denisthorn, looked blank for an instant, then regarded her servants. 'Well, that's all then, Mrs Beste, Mrs Jones. Thank you. I shall consult with his lordship about music. But I do so hope there will not be dancing in the hall.'

Mrs Beste uttered an audible sigh.

'And I do pray the chaplain from St Oswald's will not prove too old and doddery. And I shall send instruction, Mrs Beste, about removal of the carpets if dancing be the case.'

'We have tall strapping footmen.' Mrs Jones gave what passed with her as a smile. 'Two of them can roll a big carpet in a matter of minutes. And carry it away.'

'Well, isn't that why they are employed—for their physical strength, and stalwart appearance?' Mrs Beste asserted her jurisdiction. Cook had nothing to do with the footmen. It was Mr Herring the butler's bailiwick, and in his absence, that of the housekeeper, not the *cook*.

'Indeed. Thank you, ladies.'

The women in dark service clothes were replaced almost immediately by a footman, who looked slightly askew. 'His lordship would like to see you in the library, my lady.'

'Ah yes, we are due for a departure. And expecting an arrival. Formby, are you uncomfortable in that jacket? Do you have more than one pair of good gloves? I must speak to Mr Herring about liveries.' She seemed full of frustration.

The young man tugged at his jacket and looked at his boots.

'And yes, your boots too need attention. When I have spoken to his lordship, I shall need a word with Mr Herring, if you would kindly let him know.'

'My lady.'

'It must be the season. The little baron was looking a bit restricted in *his* green jacket.'

'The little baron, your ladyship?' The footman's dismayed face showed his puzzlement. 'He has ... he's been ... he is ...'

The countess looked away to the window, through which was plainly visible a sudden swift diagonal shower, which dampened leaves that only a moment ago were fluttering around. It was a dreary day in the Gloucestershire countryside. 'He is quite content to run about in the sunshine. That is all, thank you Formby.'

The footman left the room, wondering whether it was right to speak of the departed in a way that suggested they were still alive. But he would never understand people of quality. They did incomprehensible things. They confused and befuddled him. They thought a new jacket and clean gloves were more important than a good pork pie. That wearing different clothes at different times of day was mandatory. That sending each other a thousand messages a day, by post and by messenger, was more important than earnest speech, face-to-face. And his mistress thought little Frederic, who had died only a few months ago from diphtheria, was still running around in the garden playing with his hoop and stick.

Below stairs, where the real people lived, everything was as it should be. Live beings were alive, and those that had died were dead.

Chapter Two

*In which a visitor arrives from Scotland
and
Lord Croukerne expresses dismay at legislation*

He arrived at Denisthorn Hall amid a brief but upsetting instance of lack of order in the great entrance. The twin fires blazed on either side of the front door, servants came and went, and the lady of the house, accompanied by the housekeeper and butler, milled around greeting persons who departed and arrived. There were cases standing on the floor near the grand staircase, and an atmosphere of confusion underneath the renowned chandelier, which moved slightly to the movement below it.

He alighted from the carriage, ascended the stairs, and surprised everyone, perhaps pleasantly. It was a touch astonishing to observe the appearance and deportment of Mr Phineas Gow.

Denisthorn Hall was experiencing a period of change. The arrival from Scotland of Angus Crownrigg's distant uncle would have been a welcome distraction for the young man. He needed respite from learning how the estate was run. But he was caught on the horns of a dilemma, and had already left. Form demanded that since he was now Geraldine's fiancé, he had to leave the house at once. Form also dictated that a male relative call on the family to discuss his circumstance and financial situation. It was unheard of, in certain circles, for a man newly engaged not to arrange a meeting between his family and that of his fiancée.

'In the case of Cousin Angus, my dear,' Earl Croukerne had said earlier in the week to his wife Lady Edwina, when they were alone in the small sitting room, 'it is a bit out of the ordinary, because he has no family.'

'Surely he has someone to speak for him. Some distant cousin?'

'*We* are his distant cousins.'

Lady Edwina had placed crossed hands on her lap in frustration, and remained silent. Now, regarding Angus's uncle in the hall, her hitherto pessimistic expectations suddenly dissolved into a kind of relief and gladness.

Here was what appeared to be a trim neat gentleman, no less, who bowed slightly from the waist, handed his hat to a footman, stepped forward and looked her directly in the eye for only four seconds. 'Phineas Gow, Lady Croukerne. I arrive eager and prepared. The train from Edinburgh was on time.'

'Oh, welcome to Denisthorn, Mr Gow. I apologize for not coming down to the forecourt to meet you, as we are wont to do here.' She paused, looking for approval in his eye. It was there. 'There is tea in the library. The house is in a bit of disarray, as you might sense. Our daughter Geraldine has only minutes ago departed for Gallantrae.'

'As is only fitting.'

Edwina Croukerne gave him a sideways look. 'Indeed.'

'I should have liked to meet Angus's fiancée.'

She lowered her eyes. 'Of course. There will be a number of opportunities to meet. She is only at

Gallantrae, my sister's house, which is not too distant from here. Lady Margery and Sir Herbert have kindly invited Geraldine to make Gallantrae her home until the wedding. She will depart into her new life from there.'

'That is pleasing to hear. And I note my nephew Angus is already on the road.'

She paused for a beat, trying to decipher words in his heavy Scots accents. 'Ah—yes! Yes, all the fuss and bother about the engaged couple not being at Denisthorn together. It was *quite* a to-do. Now both of them are gone!'

'But how is Lord Croukerne, my lady?' He had noted the absence of the master of the house.

Her face was prim. 'I am afraid he is still being wheeled around in that awful chair.'

'Wheeled around! I was not aware.'

Surprise that Angus had not advised his uncle of Lord Croukerne's accident clouded the countess's face. 'It's been a tiring day for my husband. His man has taken him in to his room for the interim, so his apologies are tendered. He might be fine for dinner, if I move to delay it by about fifteen minutes, unless that inconveniences you.'

'Not at all. I am at your disposal. I should not dream of debating your household's plans, Lady Croukerne.'

'Thorn, his lordship's valet, will let us know. Getting used to a new wheelchair, seeing Geraldine off, expecting you from Scotland, and Cousin Angus departing for Cheltenham as well ... it has all been a bit too much, I'm afraid.'

'Oh dear.'

The countess waved a dismissive hand. 'And there's more to come. I wonder whether the household will ever settle.' She laughed. 'Athena, our older daughter, leaves for London tomorrow.'

'There is an older daughter!' Mr Gow hid his surprise with more words. 'How fortunate. How fortunate you are, indeed. And she is still with you. Ahem, that is, keeping you company.'

Lady Croukerne did not elaborate on the reason Athena was not yet married. Neither did she hint at the consternation and confusion raised by her older daughter's recent attitude. It would be the height of indiscretion and foolishness to disclose to this stranger the recent trials presented to them by her.

'Still with us, yes. Yes. We are indeed fortunate.' She cleared her throat gently as they moved into the library, whose warm and welcoming atmosphere benefitted further from the delightful scent of good tea and one of Mrs Jones's cakes on a stand. A footman stood by. 'And I trust, Mr Gow, that you ...'

'I travel without my valet, unfortunately, my lady. The story behind the reason is a sad one. But in any case, I arrive with a full set of luggage, including black ...'

'Of course.' Her ladyship did not want to discuss matters of a gentleman's wardrobe, but she supposed she had to explain arrangements in her husband's absence. 'Godwin, one of our senior footmen, will look after you, naturally. He has had a lot of experience looking after our travelling guests. We have put you in the room we call Byron.'

'You have singularly modern names for your rooms, Lady Croukerne. How extraordinary.'

Her smile was wide, and not only because her guest rolled his Rs in a strenuous fashion. 'Not that unusual, but not something the entire family approves of.' She thought of her mother-in-law, her ladyship the dowager marchioness of Harpensted, who hated the concept of naming bedrooms and suites after literary figures, and made a point of saying so. 'But to counter the monotony of naming rooms by the mere colour of their furnishings, I thought of something novel.' She tittered.

'Aha.' He laughed. 'Novel, indeed.' He took a cup of tea from the attending footman without looking at him, and turned when the doors opened to admit Lady Athena.

'May I present my older daughter. This is Mr Phineas Gow, my dear.'

'Lady Athena, I am so pleased to meet you before you set off for London. Will you be gone long?'

The ladies exchanged a brief look at the correctness of this man's bearing and demeanour, even though it was somewhat difficult to understand what he said due to his heavy accent.

'A few weeks. It's a shame the house in Belgrave is not used more, I always think. And there is a lot happening here. So I considered that leaving everyone to the preparations for Geraldine's wedding, without having to look after me as well, would not be a bad idea.'

It was clear from the look in Lady Croukerne's eyes that she held a different opinion.

'You are with us until the wedding then, Mr Gow?'

'Och, I'm afraid not, Lady Athena. I shall have to go away and return, if that is quite suitable to the household. I cannot allow my business in Glasgow and Edinburgh to proceed during a long absence. It would not only be inadvisable, but foolhardy.'

Athena's face showed a marked increase in interest. 'And what, may I ask, is the nature of your business in Scotland, Mr Gow? And does it involve Mrs Gow to any extent?'

'I am very much afraid there is no longer a Mrs Gow.'

'I'm so sorry to hear that.' Athena did not look sorry at all.

Her mother watched her changeable daughter with curiosity as she listened to their guest.

Geo Herring, butler at Denisthorn, stood in the exact spot he demanded his staff kept free and clear. He planted himself at the foot of the service stairs and drummed fingers on his waistcoat, just above the fob pocket, from where the silver chain attached to his watch dangled. In two minutes exactly, he would ascend to sound the dinner gong.

Taking a deep breath, he moved to the hearth in the servants' hall and regarded the mantel clock, which was known for its accuracy. He growled under his breath when he compared the two dials. 'No, no, no, no, no.'

'Something's wrong, Mr Herring.'

'Very wrong, Mrs Beste. I have been asked by her ladyship to delay the gong by fifteen minutes, and I now doubt my ability to do so with absolute precision.'

Her lean strong face might be seen, by anyone who did not know her, to frown. But it was a benign look, through the creases and furrows of a certain age, and the evidence of worry and travail, having executed her part of housekeeper at Denisthorn for a good number of years, and that only after having served in a number of lesser roles.

'No doubt, Mr Herring, whatever the obstacle is, it will all be put right when the family is at dinner.'

'It's my *watch*, Mrs Beste. My silver watch. It has lost a minute since dinner last night.'

'Oh, that will not do at all.' She consulted her own silver watch, which, in its own figured case, swung from a chatelaine at her waist. 'You must send it into the village right away. Could Formby not run in tomorrow morning?'

'I should have to walk down myself. I cannot imagine entrusting something as particular and valuable to a footman. Especially not Formby.' Disapproval of her suggestion rang in his voice like a tenor church bell. 'And now, in exactly ... two minutes, I must ring that gong or the family will never have dinner. It is inconceivably late as it is.'

'Yes, Mrs Jones has held back the laden dishes. The kitchen maids are waiting.'

'They can carry the first course to the servery now. Godwin, what are you doing here?'

'There is a ...' The footman saw profound irritation etched on the butler's face. 'I'm here to carry the tray of salmon up to the servery, Mr Herring. Maisie came to fetch me, as she was bade by Mrs Jones. But there is something I must say.'

'Well, you will have to say it after the gong!' The butler was halfway up the stairs to the baize door as he said the words, while replacing the precious watch in his side pocket.

'What's wrong with Mr Herring?'

'Not with him, but with his watch, Godwin. Now hurry with the salmon, or you will have to answer to Mrs Jones.'

'But perhaps you should know there is a ...'

'Go!'

It was not Godwin who wheeled Lord Croukerne into the dining room that evening. Thorn, his lordship's valet, had taken a far less frigid and uninterested stance in household matters since his master's near-fatal accident. Perhaps it was the storm of that night, or the shock the whole household had received to see the earl injured. Perhaps an internal alarm had woken the valet up. Taciturn and aloof up to then, he rarely opened his mouth, and some of the housemaids had no idea of the quality of his voice.

Now, he took over care and maintenance of the new wheelchair, which had arrived from London on the train with a man from the factory, to instruct the household on such matters. Armed with a shiny new spouted oil can, some special tools, and all manner of polishing paraphernalia, Thorn came to life.

Someone below stairs had said the valet had missed his calling, and should have been an artisan, a carpenter, a smith, or at the very least a handyman.

'Handyman! Is that a real word?'

'If you can hear it, Mrs Beste, it must be real.'

'Do not be clever with me, Simpson.' The

housekeeper had hooked an eyebrow at Lady Athena's new lady's maid and frowned severely. She had hardly been there three days, and already was making her presence felt. Her employment was the result of another of the young ladies' loud quarrels.

Lord Croukerne drew a line under it by instructing the housekeeper to interview a lady's maid.

'I am so sorry, I'm sure, Mrs Beste. But I read the word in one … in a … one of …'

'Have you been leafing through reading materials upstairs, young lady?'

It was plain there was no escape from the older woman's inquisition. Meg Simpson was not young; she was being put in her place. 'Yes, Mrs Beste. Prudhomme said there's quite a bit to learn.'

'Miss Prudhomme to you.'

'Miss Prudhomme, her ladyship's maid, has been instructing me on matters to do with knowledge and deportment, as well as systems and routines, seeing I have not long been in this house.'

'Yes—and here you are, a new maid for Lady Athena. You have scarce been here three days and must already pack off on the train. So you had better learn a lot—as much as Fairley, who is travelling to Gallantrae with Lady Geraldine. But I was sure her ladyship said you were employed as a lady's maid with an acquaintance of hers.'

'Yes, for some years, but a new lady—and a young one at that, will not be the same. And then there's this large house.'

'And did you peek inside books at your former, smaller, household, Simpson?' Mrs Beste was a bit arch.

'As a matter of fact, reading and writing are all part of it, aren't they? So I do peek inside copies of *The Ladies' Treasury* in the library.'

'And that's where you saw the word handyman. Well, do not let anyone catch you touching the family's books and things. But I do admire initiative, I must admit, and a good memory, so get along with you now.'

Thorn insisted on pushing the earl around in the wheelchair himself, so from morning until night, he was seen either fulfilling his pushing duties or caring for the chair. The earl had been moved, for the sake of personal convenience, household expediency, and access, to the small library, which had been turned into a temporary bedroom. There was a stairway cupboard close by which was turned into a wardrobe, and a small lamp room off the hall filled and fitted with a temporary bed for the valet, so Thorn found himself isolated from the rest of the staff, caring for his master's coats and shoes there, rather than in the boot room in the passage to the kitchen.

On the evening of Mr Gow's arrival, Thorn was just withdrawing from the dining room when he caught a few telling words from the earl. But since he was not one to tell tales below stairs, the concern was never to broach the ears of the servants, unlike most of the other news and information that reached the household and infiltrated it, from attics to basements.

There are no secrets at Denisthorn was a frequently uttered sentence that everyone muttered as a matter of course. In the case of Thorn, it was not a foregone conclusion.

After a brief introduction and welcome, Mr Gow

settled on Lady Croukerne's right, across from Lady Athena, who seemed flushed and animated.

'There is no smile in your eyes, daughter dear, although you seem excited.'

'Mama!' Athena disliked the observation in front of the newly-arrived relative of Angus Crownrigg. He was after all a perfect stranger.

Her father came to the rescue. 'You are no doubt anticipating your journey to London tomorrow. The train should run on time, so do get Simpson—is that her name?—to make sure you set off on time.'

'I cannot see why I should have Meg Simpson. Why did we have to take on someone entirely new? Why can't Geraldine have a new lady's maid?'

Lady Croukerne fussed with her napkin. 'We have had this conversation before. It was decided. Mrs Beste and I decided together.'

'As you see, Mr Gow,' Athena addressed the newcomer, 'I have very little say in the choice of my own girl.'

'*As you can see, Mr Gow*, household matters follow us to the dinner table these days at Denisthorn.' Lord Croukerne was apologetic. 'Down to the selection of a lady's maid.'

'I do not mind it one bit, my lord. One rather gets a feel of the quality of the household, and how efficiently it is run.'

Edwina Croukerne's head swivelled at the words. So Mr Gow was not only well-mannered and a gentleman; looking splendid, despite a balding head, despite a face which looked rather displeasing at some angles, in evening suit and black tie. He was also diplomatic and tactful, knowing how to respond in gracious words.

Athena went on. 'She is extremely efficient, and that is a fact. And she does seem to have charge of the latest fashions and hairstyles.'

'It is why she was employed, my dear. Now that Fairley is off at Gallantrae with your sister, you need looking after, and you will be in London! Goodness knows you ought to be cared for well there. You ought to look your very best.'

'But she seems interested in a number of other things.'

'I think we have heard enough of Simpson at the dinner table tonight.' Ninian Croukerne turned to their guest. 'There are other more important matters to discuss.' He turned slightly and winced at a stab of pain from his spine. 'Mr Gow, you are no doubt abreast of the upsetting legislation introduced in parliament by Sir William Harcourt last August.'

'I ... er ... ahem ... naturally.' It seemed Mr Gow felt uncomfortable.

'Well, pray do not be upset at me introducing a financial matter with ladies present and at the dinner table, of all places, but times are such, and my infirmity is such, that we might not get another opportunity. I'm sure the ladies, if they are bored, will turn to each other for conversation. If my mother, the dowager marchioness, were present, however, I do think she would join us with some eagerness, after her initial shock.'

The mention of the dowager marchioness made Mr Gow prick up his ears. Word of the redoubtable figure, her immense wealth, her two titles, and her frightening reputation had reached him when people knew he was going to Denisthorn Hall. But she was luckily absent, staying he was told at her own residence, Cheltenham House; but his lordship's manner made the visitor curious.

'Having a Liberal government is proving to be a trial.' The earl looked closely at his guest across the table. It was clear this was some kind of a test.

'Indeed. It is rocking a few boats.'

Lord Croukerne was not fully persuaded by the guarded and ambiguous riposte. The less than handsome face gave no hint of any political leaning. He went on. 'But the imposition of death duties—*death duties*, no less—is going to affect us when I ... that is, when I am no more. And affect the reason you are here, Mr Gow.'

The guest put down his fork for a pause. 'I am here for a happy reason, Lord Croukerne.'

'Of course, of course.' The earl shifted uncomfortably in his wheelchair. 'I do agree that the wedding of my daughter Geraldine to your nephew is cause for celebration. But there is also the matter of making sure Cousin Angus has a clear picture of what it involves to inherit the title and the estate. Death duties are going to make it all much more complicated. And then there is the tradition we must observe, of disclosing to each other the important estate matters that relate to the circumstances ...' He caught a look from his wife.

'When we rise, perhaps, Ninian.'

'Very good, Edwina. I shall wait for you ladies to adjourn.'

So conversation turned to hunting, shooting and

riding. It was a pity Geraldine, who could speak in great depth and detail of such things, was not present. In her stead, her father, who did not hope to ride again, held his own.

'We lost an excellent mount the night I was injured. I'm afraid my foolishness meant losing Buttercup, and she was my daughter Geraldine's favourite horse.'

There was a moment's silence.

'Our stables, however, are not to be permanently depleted. There is a new foal at Gallantrae.'

'Geraldine is sure to wangle some sort of arrangement with Uncle Herbert.' Athena's tone was arch. 'That should make her happy.'

'Wangle!' It was clear the countess did not like her daughter's choice of words.

'Would it not make a wonderful wedding gift?'

'What—a horse? I do not see how it would make any sort of a gift to anyone.' Lady Croukerne looked appalled.

'Just think of the appropriateness! Geraldine would appreciate a good bit of horseflesh much more readily than she would consider a lace tablecloth, or a Spode dinner service. Or even furnishings for an entire floor of Denisthorn Hall.' Lord Croukerne laughed and sipped his sweet wine. He was grateful for the dessert course. They dispensed with savouries for family dinners, so the gentlemen would soon be alone to discuss whatever they liked.

'I must smile at the daunting prospect of furnishing a floor of this beautiful but very large house, Lord Croukerne.'

'Oh, I was not joking, sir.' He turned to look Phineas Gow in the eye. 'I have had a long discussion with your nephew Angus. Before my accident, he was all for taking up residence with my daughter in Edinburgh, where his business is situated.'

'That would have distressed me, as you would imagine. My daughters are close to me.' Lady Edwina tilted her head.

'So you have not sought a suitable residence close by?'

'There are two, which would require too much renovation before they could be habitable by a newly-married couple. And since my accident, they both see sense in living here at Denisthorn Hall, with Cousin Angus taking over part of the management of the estate. It is an onerous and fatiguing undertaking. With this circumstance.' He gestured at his wheelchair.

'I see.' Mr Gow put down his fork once more. 'I see the sense in that. Although how a banker, as my nephew is, is to accustom himself to running an estate, is a point to consider. Is there a home farm? Are there many tenants? Do you have a good agent?' The guest stopped and lowered his eyes. 'I apologize. I cannot bombard you with questions of that nature. It is in fact none of my business.'

'Oh, but it is. I must outline to you what Angus Crownrigg, of Hawick, will inherit as heir to the title and the estate.'

'When the time comes.'

'Exactly so.'

'And it is my duty, my lord, and why I am here,' Phineas Gow continued, 'to outline to you the extent of

Angus's ... let us say, endowment. He is quite a successful young man, he leads me to believe.'

'Ah, so you have it from him directly.'

'From his lips alone. But I have gone to the trouble, for everyone's sake, to confirm with appropriate authorities, what he says about the bank, his property, and so forth.'

There was a rustle from the other side of the table and the ladies rose. The guest got to his feet, and the earl bowed from his wheelchair.

'Can we expect you in the drawing room for a brandy later, Ninian?'

'Most certainly, my dear. Allow us one small cigar.'

They lit up when mother and daughter had swept out, evening dresses glimmering in electric light, installation of which was still the envy and astonishment, because of the expense, of other stately homes in the county.

'You must taste this port wine, Mr Gow.' The earl nodded at the footman, who poured each of the gentlemen a small stemmed glass of the fortified wine.

The visitor took a sip and smiled. 'One can hardly go wrong with Taylor's.'

'Ha! Even decanted into an anonymous receptacle, it is impossible to mistake, is it not?' The earl nodded in appreciation of the fact that this was a cultured man of the world. Perhaps it said something about Angus Crownrigg, of whom they still knew precious little. But Geraldine's father did not want to jump to conclusions; even fathers and sons could prove to be different, especially these days. And this, after all, was a relative on Cousin Angus's mother's side. Still, it was pleasing to find they were not inelegant peasants.

'Because Cousin Angus is a widower, Mr Gow, it does propose ... um ... *suggest* perhaps, to my wife, if not to me, a certain delicateness of situation.'

'It was a sad affair, Lord Croukerne.'

'Of which we know very little. It did not seem appropriate to question Angus himself.'

'Let me tell you what I know of the matter. Angus and Miss Angeline Braithwaite, as she was—the second daughter of Nicholas Braithwaite—married only about four years ago in Chester.'

'Nicholas Braithwaite ... that name is not new.'

'Must be familiar, yes. He owns several Lancashire mills and has had recent enormous success exporting to, och, what we call the new world. Losing his daughter must have been devastating. She perished from influenza, and a few complications of a discreet nature.'

'A very brief and childless marriage, I understand.'

'Sadly so. Rather brief. And her considerable fortune passed to Angus, of course. She came with good investments in the stock market, as well as properties in Chester.'

'My goodness.'

'Indeed.'

The earl had heard enough for the time being. He stubbed out his cigar in a large crystal ashtray placed at his elbow by the footman and looked around for Thorn to wheel him. 'We should join the ladies.'

The earl was considering Geraldine's good fortune. Not only would she one day be countess, and mistress of Denisthorn, but from what he was told, she would be exceedingly wealthy. The future of Denisthorn Hall was assured. He entered the drawing room just ahead of Mr Gow, on account of the wheelchair, at ease with himself and in excellent humour.

CHAPTER THREE

In which Lady Athena's desires are hinted at
and
Simpson has to learn two houses

Her past had held several moments of alarm, if not fear, but she was safe now. Meg Simpson, in her mid-thirties and a spinster, was in service since she turned twelve. Starting as a starving skivvy, then a harassed laundry girl, then a scullery maid, then an upstairs maid, in an isolated house in Cornwall, she eventually found stability and pleasure in being a lady's maid, a position of some importance in a household. Some masters—and mistresses—proved to be demanding and difficult to deal with, and some servants she worked with were tribulations in their own right.

But some people she encountered and served were kind and instructive, and she still grieved for her last mistress, who died of diphtheria in the outbreak of the previous year. No longer needed at the house near Dartmoor, she sought and applied for another position, was given an excellent character, and found herself, before she had properly taken stock of her situation, at renowned Denisthorn Hall.

'So I am to be addressed by my last name, Lady Athena. I am usually called Meg.'

Athena regarded her new maid's tall sticklike appearance, her greying hair and long nose, and indicated that yes, that was the way at Denisthorn. 'I hope you find the household to your liking, Simpson. Mrs Beste will see you are accommodated suitably while we are here. In London, arrangements are rather different. It's a smaller house, but finer. A bit more grand and elaborate, since there are no hunts or house parties there. And you might not have to share a room.'

Simpson nodded. Her young mistress seemed reasonable enough. And she had already smiled at the fact that despite a grey hair or two showing under her maid's bonnet, Mrs Beste called her 'young lady'.

'So we might discuss a better uniform with Mrs Bone, who is the housekeeper at the London House. How would you like a nice shade of burgundy or bottle green? You must be rather fed up of black, black, black.' Even as she said the words, Athena felt a proprietary feeling come over her. There was something she needed to discuss with her mother.

Simpson was dismissed. She made her way along the gallery, going through and seeking the baize door, which was further along the ladies' corridor than she had thought. The service stairs were not as steep as she was used to, which made her glad, even if, because of the modernity of this household, there was no need for her to go up and down with hot water jugs, or even lamps.

The shelves in the lamp room below stairs were still crammed with all manner of candlesticks, ordinary candelabras and oil lamps. When the house was converted to electricity, with switches placed conveniently at each doorway, the family could light the way themselves, and footmen were no longer needed to spend the late afternoon making sure lamps were filled, wicks trimmed, and glass shades checked before they were lit. There was no longer a candle table at the bottom of the stairs at night, for the family and their guests to take up. Candles were only used up in the attics, where the servants had their sleeping quarters. Simpson found it rather overwhelmingly modern, and had to rearrange the timetable in her head to coincide with the routines at Denisthorn, which were decidedly easier, and seemed more manageable, than those she was used to.

'There are two sittings for meals in the servants' hall!'

Mrs Beste paused, with a pencil poised to attack her notebook once more. 'Of course. There are many of us. Those with morning duties—the housemaids especially, and the skivvies who tend the fires—do a tour of the house before they sit to their breakfast, which the kitchen girls prepare before *theirs* and that of the footmen, except for the two who see to his lordship's needs and Thorn's now that he is in a chair, and, like I said, it's complicated. It is a large household and needs to be directed closely and with a firm hand, not to mention serious attention to the clock!'

The new servant stood and listened. It was necessary for her to get as much right from the beginning as was possible. 'So there are six housemaids?'

'Five. You will tell your young lady's needs mainly to Alice and Maisie. We have two day laundry girls, who live in the village. There is an enormous drying room that leads off the boot room, and the laundry itself is just outside the kitchen at the back. Stockings are sent out, of course, but we do our own collars. You will need the help of a footman if you need anything hoisted up or down in the drying room, because those pulley ropes are the devil to tug at.'

Simpson raised a hand to cover a smile. *The devil*, indeed. 'I'll remember that. Who else is there?'

'Her ladyship has Miss Prudhomme, her lady's maid, to look after her, her *hair*, and her needs. There are two kitchen and scullery maids who live in, and two or three day kitchen girls who come in when there is a big or formal dinner, or a hunt, or a house party.'

'What about the men?'

'House staff? There are four footmen, so you must never worry about taking in letters and telegrams, or answering to sitting or drawing room bells or the front door. They are tall, strong strapping lads of course, and do all the heavy lifting, fetching and carrying, and rug rolling. There's an under-butler, called Glover, who is presently on leave, and you have met Mr Herring, the butler, of course.' She took a breath.

'My goodness.'

'Then there is Thorn, his lordship's valet. A hall boy or two come in from the village when we have guests staying—they look after bags and boots. The outside staff, that is the grooms, stableboys, gardeners, and so forth live up in the small cottages. The stable master ...'

'Do you mean the coachman?'

'We call him the stable master here. His name is Mr Mark and he lives above the tack room. Some of them have their meals here, in the servants' hall.'

'Lady Athena has come out?'

'Yes. It was a joyful time for all of us when she was

presented at court. We heard of all the proceedings at St James's Palace. Now, at the London house, you will be required to be quick and efficient, because the social calendar there runs at four times the speed and frequency as it does here in the Gloucestershire countryside, so you must be on your toes! You will be accompanied by Miss Purl. Now this is a new position for Miss Purl.' The housekeeper gave Simpson a meaningful look. 'She is to be companion and chaperone to Lady Athena.'

'She occupied another position before?'

A sad expression swept over Mrs Beste's face. 'She is a matronly lady, and was governess to the little Baron Brockworth, who ... who was taken from us just after he turned twelve.'

'Oh!'

'Diphtheria. Very, very sad.'

'Yes.' Simpson swallowed hard. Was mention of that disastrous disease never to leave her life?

'Miss Purl will more or less look after herself, in the way of dressing and arranging her hair. But you must care for her clothes and shoes, and do any necessary hemming and mending.'

'I am quite good at that.'

'Good. The house in London also has electricity, and bristles with *switches*. The bells there are ranged over the hearth in the servant's room, as they call it, and the guest bedrooms are not named after *poets*.'

Simpson formed her mouth into a silent *Ah*.

'I know there's a lot to remember, and there will be more instruction from Mrs Bone when you get to London. There is to be a guest from the beginning. Miss

Blockley, from Minsterworth, will be there. She travels with her own maid.' She leaved back in her notebook, and sighed with impatience until she found what she sought. 'Yes, her maid is called Sarah, but downstairs here she is known as Miss Blockley, of course. Since there are so many servants' rooms in London, it will not be a problem.'

'Why not? In a smaller house?'

'The attics are divided into male and female passages, of course, reached by separate winding staircases. The rooms are tiny, but there are many more than here. So Sarah will have a room separate from yours simply because it's impossible to fit two beds into one of those tiny bedrooms.'

'I must learn two households at once, it seems. Do we have an indication of how long Lady Athena will stay in London?'

'No indication at all, but ...' The housekeeper looked to the right and left of her, and lowered her voice. 'Since her younger sister is to be married, the search for a suitable husband will be foremost on her—on everyone's—mind, I should think.'

Simpson's heart sank. She anticipated a hectic season full of quick dress changes and frequent attention to hair, jewellery and accessories. She dreaded to think what Lady Athena's shoes and hems would be like after walking out on the Heath or at Kew Gardens. 'Does Lady Athena ride?'

'Not often. Lady Athena spends hours at her little desk, writing. Her sister Lady Geraldine is the one for that kind of thing. But yes, you will be required to pack one riding habit, veil, gloves, whip and boots. And do not be surprised if she takes to a bicycle.'

'Oh *dear*. One of those modern machines.'

'Yes, mud splashes, soggy stockings, scratched and scuffed shoes, and hems caught in the bicycle chain. I do not envy you one bit.' Mrs Beste gave a jolly smile.

Simpson moved away and began her next task. Her mind raced; so Lady Athena sought a husband. That confirmed a snippet of conversation she heard through a half-open door. Unable as yet to put names to voices, all she had was a female voice saying in a prim and arch way that Lady Athena was not looking for a mere match, to even out the social discomfort of having a younger sister married before her. No; she was seeking someone fabulously wealthy, incredibly rich.

To someone like Meg Simpson, to whom Denisthorn Hall was the height of luxury, a haven from the real world which was crowded, dirty, smelly and disordered, it was inconceivable to think of anything better. One of her early positions was in a filthy warren of a home, with perishing window drapes, a permanent smell of mildew, and a slovenly cook. Here it sparkled with cleanliness, with displayed wealth, with well-nourished, contented-looking staff.

Could anyone be richer? Richer than his lordship, Ninian Crownrigg, fifth earl of Croukerne, who was also Baron Brockworth and master of the estate? Richer than this place, the largest of any she had ever worked in? Richer than these ladies, who had dresses in every colour, every fabric, and every style they desired, not to mention more than *six pairs* of shoes each? It did not sound possible.

Chapter Four

In which Athena surprises Lady Croukerne
and
Mrs Beste is once more seen out with Mr Pillow

Lady Athena stepped quickly to the double doors of the library, through which her mother flounced after a middle-of-the-day consultation with the earl. 'Mama, will there be a moment?'

'Today? My hands are full. My mind has gone to mush.'

Well, that much was true. Athena held her tongue without saying what she thought about her mother's increasing forgetfulness, and allowed her mother to proceed towards her day sitting room.

'I have just spoken to your father about liveries, and his response was a litany of figures. I do not like to be spoken to about money. Money! Filthy thing that it is. I rather think your father is becoming more modern than is good for him.'

'Fancy discussing money, Mama.' Athena had caught wind of the extent of Cousin Angus's wealth.

Lady Croukerne did not detect any sarcasm in Athena's tone. 'And with me! I do agree.'

'Five minutes, perhaps?'

The countess whirled around, setting her skirts swinging. 'My dear Athena.' Her face softened. 'Oh, Athena dear. You will soon leave for London, and our daily meetings will end. You cannot fathom, I am sure, how much I anticipate that I shall miss you.'

'Not at breakfast.' Athena meant it as a joke. Lady Croukerne was rarely seen before eleven. She had breakfast brought up, and chatted with Prudhomme while she ate, was dressed, and composed herself for the day.

'I shall miss our luncheons. And your funny brief sentences and exclamations will be missed at dinner. Your Papa will look across at your empty place and frown. Of that I am entirely sure.'

'But you will soon have Geraldine back, and with her, Cousin Angus.'

The countess held a hand to a cheek as she entered her sitting room and found her corner seat, which looked out upon the west garden.

'Oh! How am I ever going to get used to Geraldine as a married woman? She too will have her breakfast taken up. And all Papa will have ... he will have *Angus*. I do wonder whether ...'

'Mama.'

'I do wonder whether they will save any scrambled eggs for Frederic.'

'Mama!' Athena was just as aghast at her mother as the servants when they heard her speak of her young son as if he were still alive.

'Now sit by me and tell me quickly.' She took her daughter's hand. 'Was there something you wanted to discuss? Are you completely clear about how you should deport yourself in London?'

'Well, there are far too many houses to call on, on your list. Do we have such a number of acquaintances in

London? I shall only call on ladies I have met, or at least heard of!'

'You can only gain introductions to gentlemen through cultivation of acquaintance with the ladies. It's essential. You must pay visits, but only after you have left your card. Have you seen to having nice ones made?'

'I have cards.'

'And remember the fifteen-minute rule, my dear. Never over-stay your hostess's hospitality. Never bore anyone with a long afternoon visit.'

'I shan't.'

'And when you receive calls at the Belgrave house, you must be gracious and generous, and not speak only about yourself.'

'I shan't. But I must ask about the running of Belgrave.'

'Mrs Bone sees to the running of the house!'

'But am I to act as lady of the house? From whom will Mrs Bone take her orders? The house will be open. Mrs Bone will have a working staff, rather like when we are there for the season.'

'Papa comes and goes to the House of Lords. He will be in charge when he is in London. The butler there, Bone, is rather good. When Papa is absent ...' She turned, looked her daughter in the eye, and raised a hand to gently hold her chin. 'Look me in the eye, my dear. Oh, you are such a lady now, presented and all, with the world before you. Promise me, now.'

'What on earth could there be for me to promise?'

'Promise me you will speak in proper sentences.'

Lady Athena sighed. 'I do believe London is entirely full of suitable matches, Mama, if that is what you mean.'

'Make a match. Make a lovely solid match, my dear. Be sure to be in rapid communication with your father. All permissions must be correctly sought, unless you are to collect a nasty note.'

'I shall not make myself a reputation, Mama. I shall be using a lot of time for writing.'

'Writing! No! You must seek someone. A kind and considerate man … like Papa.'

'I should seek someone who has inherited a decent estate, a sizeable fortune, or has built one for himself.'

'Athena!'

'Surely you see my position, Mama. Geraldine is to be Lady Croukerne one day in the future. Where does that leave me, her older sister?'

'I thought you were happy she accepted Cousin Angus.'

'I am—of course I am, and shall continue to be happy. I had no designs on him, let me be clear on that.'

'But now …'

'Now, I must make a reasonably wealthy marriage. If I make any less a suit, I should be known as the poor sister. Aunt Margery will laugh me out of the county.'

'That is utter nonsense! My sister would not dream of such a thing.'

'In any case, we do know London is full of rich men.'

'My goodness. Whatever will I hear next?' The countess raised both hands and let them fall again.

'I have enough to wear to avoid being inconspicuous at Almack's. Everyone will be at Almack's. I should strive not to fade into the wallpaper.'

The countess replaced her hands in her lap, frustration making her tremble for a second. 'Oh, do not make a fool of yourself at the assembly rooms, Athena! We should be the talk of the entire country if you do that.'

'Is it not exactly what the assembly rooms are for, Mama? How are men and women to meet and make each other's acquaintance if there were no such places?'

'I should think that your mother's house is the most appropriate place.'

'I am off to London now. This household has seen too much disruption lately for any proper social gatherings. Why, we have not had much to do at all in the way of socializing since the little hunt last year. My stay with Aunt Margery at Gallantrae was the highlight of the entire twelve months.'

'And your coming out? Being presented at court?'

'And that.'

'And was our company so boring? We did not have anyone as interesting as that Mr Alistair Updike to stay, I suppose. Do you still write to him?'

'You know very well that I do, Mama. You scrutinize the envelopes of my post closely twice a day.'

'Oh Athena!'

'Oh, Mama.' She rose, turned, and turned again, as if changing her mind about something. 'So I am to be in charge of the London household in Papa's absence?'

'I suppose so. You will have Miss Purl there, and Miss Blockley. It will all run correctly if you remember your deportment, demeanour, good habits, and all you have learned here. You can receive calls on Thursday afternoons, like we do when the season is on, of course.

Keep your companions close. Do not set tongues wagging.'

'I plan for it not to be as ... it will be a slight bit more entertaining there, I do hope.'

'So the likes of Sir Neville Robarts will not darken your threshold.'

There was a quick intake of breath from Athena. 'Sir Neville! I had completely forgotten about him.'

'Who could forget his face? I do believe he is the ugliest of gentlemen.'

But Athena was not listening. She moved to the window and stared out at the grey weather. The garden looked depleted and sad. 'Nothing is sadder than the west garden in winter, I do declare.' She said the words automatically, turning to her mother with a bright smile.

'Oh, Athena.'

'Thank you, dear Mama. You have quite given me a brilliant, um ... a few good indications of how the London house should run.'

Lady Croukerne watched her daughter leave the room. Her eyes went to the window. She stood and watched, thinking that Frederic would run past with a ball or one of the hounds. Perhaps he would like a bicycle.

Spotless. The carpet in Mr Herring's office was spotless. Formby stood on it in front of Mr Herring's desk far more often than any of the other footmen. Hands clasped behind his back, he waited for the usual diatribe.

It came in the form of a gentle rebuke. 'Your appearance has been noted as being wanting, Formby.'

The young man tugged at his jacket.

'Don't destroy your livery in such a manner. You pull at your jacket, you wear out the fingers of your gloves, you are obviously wearing each shirt longer than three days. You do not correctly tie your stock. What is the matter with you, son? Her ladyship has complained about your appearance.'

Son? Something had got into Mr Herring. Where was the severe scolding he was expecting? 'Nothing is the matter with me, Mr Herring.'

'You know very well that is not true. You wear out gloves faster than any of the other boys. Look ,' the butler stood, chose a key from his bunch and walked the footman towards a linen cupboard built into the passageway wall. 'You know *very well* I try to open this cupboard as infrequently as possible.' He pulled out a long flat box, selected a pair of white gloves, counted the pairs that were left, closed and locked the door, and turned to face the recalcitrant footman.

'New gloves?'

'I do this to make her ladyship happy, not you, Formby. Not you. She protested about your apparel. Your gloves, and your boots. Now see that you polish those boots. Have them mended if need be. But polish them, boy. Let me see my face in them next time I see you.'

Formby regarded the gloves with something approaching amazement. Lady Croukerne must be changing. She barely used to notice him, let alone his clothing or appearance. 'I didn't think her ladyship knew I existed.'

'Don't be impertinent now. Off with you and make sure you get a haircut the next time you are in the village. And a shave! And get Mrs Beste ...'

'Mrs Beste spends a lot of time in the village herself.'

'*Formby.*'

'It's true, sir. She sits in those blue tearooms with the man from the shop. Mr Pillow, I think he is.'

'Formby. You do know I do not abide gossip among the staff. No gossip in the household, from the village, from Cheltenham House, or any other location, for that matter.'

The footman shifted from foot to foot, seeing a glimmer in the butler's eyes that had nothing to do with deportment in the household. 'But there are no secrets at Denisthorn Hall.'

'No buts. I do insist on the gossip rule.'

'Is it still gossip if it's true, sir? That's what I need to know.' Formby had a mischievous look in the eye. 'I need to know what gossip really means, sir.'

Despite his anger and dismay, the butler stopped outside his office. 'Off with you, Formby. Off with you now. I much rather prefer to hear you at the piano than tittle-tattling.' He could have bitten off the boy's head, as he had done in the past, but he was told by Lady Croukerne that Formby had to be valued, trained, made to feel he was a favoured member of the staff, for she had seen something in him that most people missed.

What that something was, the butler mused, must be a great mystery. But her ladyship saw something in him, and her word had to be observed.

CHAPTER FIVE

In which Lady Geraldine settles at Gallantrae and gains an eagerness for land and farming
and
A scandal in Lady Margery's house is narrowly avoided

Her 'reign' was behind her now, well in the past, but the dowager marchioness always swept through the grand hall at Denisthorn as if she were still lady of the house. She remembered her time there in detail, when the butler and housekeeper were staid and strict, and things ran differently. She also remembered the disasters, the misadventures, and the gossip. Gossip, gossip. There are no secrets at Denisthorn Hall. Huh! But also, many of the disastrous secrets were far behind her now.

'Ah, Edwina my dear. How lovely of you to have me to luncheon!'

'Maman, welcome.' If Edwina had her way, she would call her mother-in-law Grand-mama, as she used to when the children were little, but she had been frowned at quite plainly once, when Athena turned thirteen, so she never did it again. 'Neither of the girls are here, I'm afraid, and Ninian and I are rather rattling around in this old pile.'

'There will be crowds for the wedding, I should imagine.'

Edwina led her around to her day sitting room.

'Surely we are not lunching in here?'

'No, I thought it would be rather fun for us to sit out on the terrace. Ninian has had a very nice cane suite sent up on the train. It has specially upholstered pillows and cushions. I cannot wait for you to see it, Maman.'

'Oh. And what, pray, is going to protect our complexion from the sun?' The dowager marchioness looked horrified. 'I still suffer from, you know, backache every now and then.'

They proceeded through open French doors, whose curtains fluttered a little in a breeze that also ruffled the mirror lake, a corner of which they could just see around the side. 'Look, we have enormous parasols!'

'On enormous poles. Will they not sail off on the wind?' The older lady was astonished to see such garden furniture.

'Oh, I do hope not. I think the men have weighed them down with sandbags or some such arrangement.' Edwina settled the dowager in one of the new deep cane chairs, slipping a cushion behind her back. 'How does that feel? Are they not the most comfortable chairs?'

'It feels rather foreign! Colonial—why, they must have these exact same chairs in India!'

A footman adjusted an umbrella so it shaded the old lady completely from the sun, which was not quite directly overhead. Some shade was thrown by the side of the building.

'Oh, I do declare this to be quite amusing. I was full of trepidation, Edwina, when you said luncheon on the terrace. I imagined some kind of *picnic*.' She regarded the exquisitely laid table, whose cloth fell to the flagstones. It bore several silver-domed dishes and the Croukerne china, together with crystal glasses and monogrammed cutlery. The cream linen was crisp and perfectly folded.

Edwina laughed again. 'Oh, no. I should not dream of subjecting you to any discomfort. This is no picnic.' She gave a little titter.

'Is Ninian joining us?

'Swinnart is playing up. Ninian has a meeting with him.'

The old lady wagged a finger. 'I have told my son several times that having a recalcitrant agent is detrimental to the estate. And that Swinnart is a veritable talking machine! I wonder Ninian can sift through all the words to get to the core of whatever problems and solutions the man talks about.'

'Thousands of words.'

'Now let us discuss the wedding. Geraldine's wedding is going to be the most important event in the Cheltenham district for some time. It ought to go well.'

'It must go well, Maman.'

The modern fittings and amenities at Gallantrae had Geraldine in quite a trance. The house blazed with expensive electric light at night. Her Aunt Margery and Uncle Herbert also seemed to have twice as many servants than at Denisthorn, and a social calendar that was four times as busy. It did appear as though they had a permanent house party, drilling its clamoured course through the weeks.

'Do you always, that is, frequently have house guests, Aunt?'

'Oh, exceedingly often. Do not tell her, but I find

my sister Edwina, your mother, a touch stuffy and staid. I love a lively household. It keeps me occupied and entertained. And ...' she smiled '... it does keep the servants on their toes. Besides, what on earth would we do otherwise with more than twenty bedrooms?'

'Lively it certainly is.'

'Ah—you are speaking of tonight's soiree. Yes. We have some chamber music in the hall downstairs. That should be rather lovely. A string quartet from London. I should imagine the musicians are already here, preparing their instruments or whatever it is musicians do. You should consider musical evenings when you establish yourself properly as a married woman at Denisthorn. Shake the household up a bit! Does your fiancé Angus like music?'

Geraldine grimaced. 'I don't know. I have no idea. Ooh! I know very little about him, Aunt Margery.'

'And he about you, I should imagine. That is what the first year of marriage is for. You will get to know a great deal about, ah ... each other. And married life in *general*. If you know what ... no, you would not. Could not. I mean, the first year of married life is nothing but an eye-opener. That is, *instructive.* '

'If he is anything like Papa ...'

'I doubt anyone is quite like your father. Ninian is a model husband. In that regard, my sister is exceedingly fortunate. It does not make for a sparkling social life, I grant you, however. It must be quite dull sometimes at Denisthorn. Like I said ...'

'... I must shake it up.'

'Now do you have something suitable to wear tonight? That light brown silk makes you look rather sallow. Have you nothing a bit more um, bright?'

'Spotted yellow? I persuaded Mama to let me have a printed muslin from India. I find it rather jolly.'

'Does she still insist on you girls sweeping the floors with long voluminous skirts?'

'Our seamstress's new assistant is rather *en courant* of the latest fashions. Our hems have come up all of two inches.'

Lady Margery heaved a small sigh of relief. 'And yellow sounds much better, my dear girl. Now, I hear Angus Crownrigg has returned to Edinburgh?'

'No—he is in Cheltenham. I had a letter from him by the last post yesterday. He is exploring the possibility of opening a bank office there. He calls it a branch.'

'A branch? Explain, dear. You speak in such brief sentences.'

'He wants it to be the modern model of a bank, doing mostly—what did he say?—commercial banking.'

'And? Explain!'

'Oh, look, I am only repeating his written words. I don't know what any of it means.'

They met Sir Herbert in the hall, on their way to the dining room.

'I heard your last words, Geraldine. Very, very interesting. I think your fiancé has his head screwed on the right way, if he means merchant banking. There is a big future for anyone with enough verve, nerve, and stomach to keep up with what is going on in development and industry and to understand what is happening in America. What is happening with the gold standard.' He lifted a finger and looked excited, 'And the monetization of silver. Remember those two things.'

'Oh, Uncle Herbert—it is in fact quite a puzzle to me at present.'

'Read the papers.'

'*Really*, Herbert. The papers?'

'Margery, she must try to understand the financial news coming to us from the United States, and support her future husband with some understanding of what he will grapple with.'

'Oh, dear!'

'You are an intelligent young woman, Geraldine dear.' Margery gave an encouraging smile. 'And surely women nowadays are intelligent enough.'

'Women nowadays should do exactly what they choose, in the same way as men.' Geraldine started confidently, and ended lamely. 'At least, it's what I'm led to believe.'

Her aunt regarded her from a distance. 'You are as unlike your sister Athena as it is possible to be.'

'If they are to avoid those being mere words, young women like you need to be ready to take up the concepts of industrialization, of commerce. And do so wholeheartedly, and with a lot of intelligence and hard work. Even I do not understand all the aspects of banking—merchant, commercial, or otherwise—but they are invented by men. By people, by humans, I mean. So those with an ounce of brains and intestinal fortitude should be able to grasp them. Think of that, my dear.'

'Yes, Uncle Herbert.'

They sat at the table and were served lunch quickly by two footmen, and then left to their own resources.

She noted Sir Herbert drank only water at lunch. He wolfed down two large slices of cold roast beef accompanied by a great deal of horseradish sauce, boiled potato, sliced tomato, and buttered bread.

Geraldine did not want to stare, but she watched him help himself to more roast beef. He ate as fast as he talked, and then threw down his napkin, sighed, and pulled out his watch. At table; it was a beautifully carved gold affair with a similarly spectacular chain. But pulling a watch out at table? Her father would not have dreamed of doing such a thing. 'You are quite busy, Uncle Herbert.'

'Today we are on horseback, inspecting the hedgerows. Miles and miles of hedgerows. If England is not to have a festering problem with vermin and diseases of roots and foliage, we are to put a lot of work into conservation.' He nodded at his wife. 'Your aunt Margery knows that hedges need to be pruned every three years, and laid every fifteen or so, if they are to remain thick enough to be boundaries for livestock. And that is the work facing us at the moment. Which of them to lay, how many miles of conservation work, how to deal with vermin. It is enjoyable work if one sees the logic and reason behind it.'

'What about birds, their nests, squirrels ...'

'Aha! Beetles, bats, bumblebees! You show good sense. Pruning and laying of hedgerows is always staggered, and done with the idea of preserving wildlife and where it lives. That is, what the wildlife needs in the way of natural habitat. Owls ... hazel dormice ... hedgehogs ... Their homes must only be disturbed sensitively, leaving them enough room for not just survival, but *continuation* of what naturalists now call their lifecycles.'

This was by far more interesting than banking. Geraldine perked up. 'How fascinating! I must take more interest in the hedgerows at Denisthorn.'

'You have miles of fencing down there, because of a number of historic aspects, and also the lay of the land. Your grandfather, the fourth earl, installed fences and stiles, stiles and fences. I suppose it was the right expedient in some fields and meadows when the land was subdivided to create Gallantrae. But yes—the stretch behind the top cottages, above Grayson's Mound and the lesser meadow, has a beautiful stretch of ancient hedgerow, mostly composed of guelder rose, spindle, and hawthorn, which borders the road to Brockworth.'

'I do wish to learn more about my own home.'

'Get your father or his agent to show you the plans and maps. Start from there, my dear.'

'Yes, Uncle. I thought I knew my home, but I see there's a lot more to learn.' Geraldine looked into Sir Herbert's face. She saw something in his eyes that bordered on admiration. Was she mistaken? She could not let go the excitement, which glimpses of the future showed her. It was enticing and gave her a good feeling. She and Angus would ride the perimeters of Denisthorn with some pride, if their work was seen to benefit the estate and prepare for the years ahead. In her mind's eye, she rode by her husband's side, and her engagement to Angus Crownrigg started to feel good, thrilling, and worthwhile for perhaps the first time.

The string quartet played some antiquated music, but also some modern pieces Geraldine did not recognize.

She noted that Schumann and Rubenstein, announced by the quartet leader, were popular. The carpet had been rolled away where three or four ranks of chairs were set out, and some step-dancing followed.

Even though Aunt Margery strove to be modern, she was reluctant to let step dancing go. 'Any opportunity for a bit of a dance, I say!' She was happy with the evening, even though it was small and intimate, with fewer than twenty people present.

Geraldine was encouraged to dance, and accepted an invitation from young Major Fortescue, of the new Gloucestershire Regiment. She was not adept at step dancing, and hazarded to say so.

'But neither am I, Lady Geraldine. I suspect everyone will be thinking of their own feet, so little attention will be paid to ours.'

'How gallant, Major.'

He moved away after the music stopped, but later on offered to bring Geraldine a glass of sparkling white wine.

'Thank you, yes.'

'The quartet is going to attempt a quadrille. Might I have the honour once more?' The handsome soldier bent slightly from the waist, and flashed serious dark grey eyes.

Geraldine took his hand, thinking nothing of it, and missing the expression on Lady Margery's face. Her aunt stood by the hall door, talking to a small group of ladies. While Geraldine and Major Fortescue danced, she moved away to stand on her own at some distance from the musicians.

She started to make her way towards her niece, but

an interruption from the butler made her pause.

'Mister Angus Crownrigg.' Cotterell, the butler, had a high-pitched voice which made everyone pause to look at the newcomer he announced.

'Cousin Angus!' Geraldine did not expect to see him there.

He made his way to Lady Margery, who was quickly joined by Sir Herbert.

'I'm afraid I call on you at this hour without invitation, Lady Margery ... Sir Herbert. I was told of your soiree and thought I might abandon all restraint and politeness, and throw myself upon your hospitality.'

'I was only saying earlier today, Mr Crownrigg, that I love a lively household.' She smiled graciously at Angus. 'And although it's not an open house all the time, we do appreciate a visit from a future neighbour.' Was there a subtle rebuke in her riposte?

Geraldine had started towards Angus, but stopped when she realized it would be more proper for him to seek her out. She moved back from the middle of the hall, where people were still dancing, and took up a position where she thought Angus would be sure to notice her.

It was Aunt Margery who eventually came up to draw her toward the new arrival.

'Geraldine.' He inclined his head slightly and took her offered hand.

'Angus.'

'You seem to be enjoying your stay at Gallantrae.'

'Oh, very much so. My aunt and uncle have made me welcome, and they do indeed have a lively household.'

'So I see.' He turned away and said a few words to the gathered guests.

Geraldine waited, feeling unusually awkward and shy.

Her fiancé seemed in high spirits. 'Ah, the music has started again.' He placed his glass on the tray of a passing footman, after hardly having had a sip. 'Lady Margery, if I might be so bold?' He turned towards Geraldine's aunt, but she had moved away a few seconds before, to have her place taken by Mrs Jonathan Pembridge, from Ewlyn House, a lady to whom he had been introduced a few seconds ago. 'Mrs Pembridge?'

The lady looked puzzled, but took his arm and Angus led her away to dance in the middle of the hall, where three other couples were moving to the music. It came to an end rather quickly. Angus kept the lady talking in the middle of the floor, and they resumed dancing when the quartet struck up again.

It was plain that Sir Herbert did not like Angus's behaviour.

And Geraldine, feeling ignored and slighted, heard a whisper behind her.

'Where does he think he is—at the Alexandra music hall? Who is this man?'

'Obviously someone more habituated to the Glasgow halls, as you say! Ha ha!'

With some relief, Geraldine saw the evening was coming to an end and people were leaving.

'You must go up, now, my dear.' All of a sudden Aunt Margery spoke primly and archly. 'You cannot be seen to linger in Angus's presence. His carriage will likely be brought round soon. Off you go.'

'Aunt ...?'

'Geraldine, my dear. Perhaps you do not follow the rules at Denisthorn, or are not aware of them, but first you dance *twice* with the same gentleman; you, a young lady who is engaged to be married, might I add. And then Angus arrives, and does not dance with you, but *twice* with a lady he has just set eyes on!'

'Is that not ...?'

'Of course it is *not*!'

Chastened, Geraldine hurried up to her room, and found herself not bursting into tears, which she had feared on the way up, but trying to cool and soothe her red cheeks, which in the mirror looked as if they glowed more than the candles on her dressing table, for which there was no real use, since the electric lamps were on.

'Oh, Fairley! I shall never understand some things.'

Her maid took charge, and hastened to get Geraldine ready for bed.

'It's a long time since dinner, my lady. Don't be upset. Shall I ring for some cocoa or warm milk?'

'At this hour? No—I shall dip into the biscuit jar. And I do entreat you to pour me a glass of water. That should suffice.'

'Water? Yes, my lady, if you are sure.'

'Mr Crownrigg and I have set tongues wagging, I'm afraid.'

'An engaged couple might often run that danger, my lady. I am sure it's nothing unusual. Nothing these people have never seen before.'

'No, Fairley. It's not the case this time. I should agree with you if we had caused a scandal together. But he got tongues wagging for one reason, and I for another.

Quite separately.'

From what Fairley had already heard from one of the footmen, tongues would be wagging for some time.

'It will not prove hard to live down, perhaps.'

'I don't know, Fairley. I truly do not know. I preferred the afternoon, when I read a book about Gloucestershire, its towns, villages, and countryside.'

'So do you feel perhaps, my lady, that his arrival was a bit inopportune?'

'We are not supposed to be thrown together too much until our wedding day. But something told me he was here for the entertainment. The dancing, the ... the guests, and perhaps not for my company alone.'

'I see.' The maid waited for Geraldine to hand her the stockings she pulled from her feet. 'I see.'

CHAPTER SIX

In which Denisthorn Hall suffers an invasion
and
the under-butler returns

Calm and quiet. Tranquil and still it was, below stairs at Denisthorn Hall. Mrs Jones stood at her wall desk making a list, and two footmen smoked by the fire, having just descended from opening and closing the shutters in the high attic drying room for the girls to clean behind, carrying out two rugs to be beaten, and distributing the morning post.

'It should feel like there's less to do with Lady Athena in London, and Lady Geraldine up at Gallantrae. But I feel flattened.'

'What—they're working us too hard, ye think, Godwin?'

'We all have our tasks worked out for us. Even his lordship's dog gets walked by the same boot boy every day. It's not that. Perhaps I'll feel better when Mr Glover comes back.'

'I can't get used to calling him mister.'

'He's been under-butler a fair while. Bet you anything his back and thighs don't ache like this, 'specially not after a rest. Where's he gone?'

'To his family in Leicester.'

'If it's your thighs ... oh, ye chump, Godwin.'

'What?'

'Weren't you kicking a ball around for hours with the dairy boy?'

'Not hours. But now you remind me, yes, and I hadn't played ball for years.'

'It's yer muscles telling you something. That you're getting old!'

'I'm hardly older than that Mr Angus.'

'*God-win*!' The butler's booming voice came through the door to the passage. '*That* Mr Angus? I think you had better temper how you speak about the family. Mr Crownrigg is his lordship's cousin.' Mr Herring's fierce eyes bulged out of a bony face that started to redden with anger.

'Distant cousin, we hear.'

'No matter how close or distant, one word must be said, and one word from me is enough—*respect*!'

'Yes, Mr Herring.'

'Now hop upstairs and collect all the letters from the tray in the hall and run them down to the post office. There are quite a few today.'

'Can't Formby?'

One brief look at the butler's face was enough to silence Godwin and send him clattering up the service stairs.

He found chaos in the great hall. Lady Croukerne, her lady's maid, and the dowager marchioness stood in a huddle in the middle of the beautiful Turkish carpet. They all held their skirts up, just short of it not being an alarming fact in itself; with distressed looks on their faces, and all chattering at once.

'Oh, my goodness me!'

'Oh! Oh! Oh, what was that?'

'You know very well what it was, Edwina!'

'Gracious! Goodness! How is it possible?'

'Godwin! Ah! Oh! Thank goodness you're here!'

The footman took a step back. 'What is it, my lady?'

'Oh! Oh! Oh!'

There were a few more little screams, and a rumbled complaint from his lordship, who sat in his wheelchair, without his hound, for once. 'Godwin, do something about it. Right now!'

'About ... ?' But it was unmistakeable. It was plain what the problem was; what it was that caused such noise and confusion in the great entrance of Denisthorn Hall.

The ladies once more lifted their skirts, ran towards the library doors and uttered subdued screams.

'Godwin!'

'Godwin!'

'Right away, your lordship.' But he did not know what to do.

There, scampering across and around the silk carpet, were no less than four tiny grey mice.

The under-butler stepped without a sound up the narrow uncarpeted stairs to the manservants' corridor, having arrived through the service entrance, leaned against the door of his room, lest it creaked, and gently turned the knob. Settling a battered suitcase on the foot of the iron bed, he sat next to it and exhaled greatly, then combed fingers through his curly shock of reddish hair.

'Phew.' He toed and heeled off his boots, and lay back across the width of the bed. 'It's over. I'm back. *It's over.*' He closed his eyes for a moment.

'Glover! Mr Glover, I mean.' Someone shook him by the shoulder.

Glover opened his eyes. The room was dark. A spectre bearing a small candlestick stood over him. 'What is it?' He slurred his words, sitting up. 'Who is it? Who are you? What *time* is it?'

'You're back, Mr Glover.' It was Formby, who lit three other candle stubs from the flame of the one he brought.

'Evidently. It's freezing up here. Is that you, Peter?'

'Yes, it's me.'

The under-butler stood. 'What are you doing in here? This is my room and Godwin's.'

'Bob Godwin is in trouble below stairs. Well, not in trouble, exactly. He's occupied. I'm here to fetch ...' He rifled and rustled through one of the drawers in the chest Glover shared with the senior footman.

'Don't go through our drawers! What do you want?'

'Gloves, he needs a clean pair of gloves.'

The under-butler pulled him away from the chest of drawers. 'You won't find them here. You know where the clean gloves are kept. Mr Herring keeps a hawk eye on that box. Down near the row of hooks, under the stairs. Right next to the aprons. You know this. Everyone knows this. What's gotten into you, Peter?'

'Didn't think you'd be back. They said you'd be gone a month.'

'So you're pinching my gloves! What time is it?'

'The family is in the drawing room. Dinner is over.'

'Good heavens. It's past nine. I've slept almost two hours.' He raked his hair and sat back on the bed. 'I'd better get myself organized.'

'Nothing to keep you with your family, then? You just can't stay away from work, can ye?'

The older man regarded the footman and shook his head. 'Family—bah! You know what families are like, Pete. Hatches, matches, and dispatches.'

'Hmm?'

'Births, marriages and deaths.'

'Oh.'

'There I was, thinking it would be a happy matter of attending my brother's wedding.'

'Yes, happy. And?'

'And, Pete. Two ands and a but.'

Even in dim flickering candlelight it was plain young Formby did not gather what Glover meant. His face looked blank.

'I also attended my father's funeral, and two of my sisters had babies.'

'All while you were there ... what, in the space of a fortnight?'

'Nigh on three weeks.'

'Sorry to hear about yer da.'

'Well, he went. Just like that.' Glover snapped fingers. 'The day after the wedding. And I had no idea Libby and Peg were in the family way. No one tells me *anything*.'

'You did get a letter about the wedding.'

'Hmm.'

'Isn't Peg the one who got married? Just in time, then!' He smirked.

Glover shooed him away. 'Don't get all moral and upright with me. I'm just as much detached from it all as you are.'

'I don't know any of these people.'

'Exactly. *Exactly*, I say. Neither do I, it seems. Out of my way.'

Formby sniffed. 'Ye don't have to be so gruff about it. I know yer da has just passed, but hey.'

'I must see Mr Herring about wearing an armband. It's here somewhere. Hasn't been long since we wore them for young Baron Brockworth. Where's Godwin? What's keeping him *occupied*?'

Formby laughed. 'Laying traps.'

Glover turned from the drawer.

'There's a plague of mice in the grand hall.'

'What! Have the family seen any?' Glover's jaw dropped.

'The family's stood on chairs with skirts held up, all afternoon, if Godwin's to be believed. The shrieking was something awful. Godwin said he'd been trying to tell Mrs Beste and Mr Herring for days. No one listened.'

CHAPTER SEVEN

In which a proposal is received
and
Lady Geraldine is overwhelmed by attention

They kept coming; lilies, chrysants, carnations and roses. Some in casual posies, others in ornate, artfully created bouquets. Two upstairs maids ascended with arms full of flowers, eyes wide with wonder. Gallantrae House had never been inundated in quite such a floral flood.

'Please, please. Shona, could you just put them in water and put them about the house?'

The maid bobbed assent and turned, halfway down the stairs. 'They be from ...'

'From Mr Crownrigg, I know.' She did not know whether to smile or show her confusion and distress in a heartfelt frown. There was no time to think, or even turn on the threshold of the day sitting room.

For her aunt had already overtaken the descending maids. 'Geraldine! How wonderful. How astonishing! Could all these flowers be from Angus?' She swept in past Geraldine in a gust of spotted green georgette and eau de cologne, unfastened her great straw hat and flung it onto a settee. 'You must feel so loved.'

Geraldine did not know how to feel. 'It must be an apology of some kind. Perhaps Cousin Angus felt his behaviour was untoward.'

'He is a young man in love, my darling niece.

Young men do all sorts of stupid things, lacking foresight and opprobrium as they do, compared to us women. Surely you forgive him for dancing with ... who was it he danced with? I forget now. See? We all forget, and you should too.' She took Geraldine's hand and looked into her eyes.

'I don't know what to think, Aunt Margery.'

'Don't think. Don't think. A note will arrive presently, of that I am in no doubt.'

'I have had three notes already. One at breakfast and now another two.'

'See? And these, dear girl,' Lady Margery stopped at a vase of near-perfect chrysanthemums, a cluster of bright yellow pom-poms arranged among maidenhair fern. 'These are hothouse flowers. He must have spent a fortune on you. Do you not feel gratified and spoilt? That's how you feel! Pampered and cossetted.' The usually sensible aunt gushed.

Geraldine sat by the window. Down on the gravel drive, she could see another florist's boy turn the corner to the service entrance. 'There are more on the way. I wish it would stop.'

She could not be sure if her aunt had heard the words she spoke out loud. She dropped her chin into a hand, looking at the florist's boy progress to the side of the house on the gravel drive below. Why was she not as thrilled as Aunt Margery thought she should be about all this attention from Angus? She did not know anything about engagements, or relationships, or, if the truth were to be known, about men. She was not sure she even liked them. She squeezed her eyes shut and wondered whether she liked Cousin Angus, and if what she was doing was sensible and a good thing to do with her life.

'Shouldn't I rather be astride a horse galloping over the hills with Mark?'

Aunt Margery heard her this time. 'What are you saying, Geraldine? No lady rides astride a horse. And who on earth is Mark?' She placed a hand on her niece's shoulder, making her turn slightly away from the window. 'You cannot have ridden astride, ever! And I repeat, who is Mark? Do I know him? Does your mother know him? More to the point, does Angus, or your father, know this *Mark*?'

It would have been pure insanity to mention to Aunt Margery that Mark was not a man, but one of the grooms at her father's stables; a young woman, Mary Mark, the daughter of one of the retainers, who so loved horses and riding she took up the duties of stableboy. She mucked out stables, cleaned tack, prepared mounts and generally made herself useful in the purpose-built outhouses that Lord Croukerne had inherited from his father and rather tended to ignore, if it weren't for the usefulness of the carriages. Transport was an important thing; how would they get about without the brougham, the little gigs, and the wagonettes? How would they cope without stables and horses and all the trappings? How could she cope without horses, without Mark?

'Answer me, will you, Geraldine!'

'It was fanciful, Aunt Margery. Um ... I wondered what it might be like to be a man.'

'A man!'

'And care about little else than riding and shooting and wandering all over a large estate.'

'And Mark ...?'

'It's only one of the attendants at Papa's stables, with duties I rather envy right at this minute.'

'How could you envy that?'

'Helping riders mount, sweeping, pushing a barrow of hay ... of ... of muck.'

The older woman held the back of one hand to her forehead. 'You cannot be serious! Oh dear!' She chuckled aloud. 'I thought for an instant that you might be serious.' She laughed again. 'You are suffering from anxiety about your forthcoming wedding. You're taking to heart what your uncle said about looking after the estate. It's perfectly natural. Talk to me in a year, my girl, and I shall note your sense of contentment and joy.'

'Really!'

'Yes, really. You would not in the slightest want to be a man, with all the concerns of a large estate heaped on your ... on your ... well, not only on your desk, but also on your shoulders. Men are not like us. They positively enjoy all the problems with tenants and farming and crops and cattle! Well, at least I hope so, because it is all that which keeps the entire world going round.' She seemed so sure of how the world worked. 'I hasten to add your life would be a lot different if it were not for your father's work, and that of the previous earls, who have managed all his land, for generations. And thank heaven for Angus, who will inherit all the glory of it.'

'And the expense, and the work, and the problems.'

'Leaving you, like all other ladies, to charitable works and management of the household. It works perfectly!'

'Perfectly.' Geraldine's word was dull, a mere repetition of the sound without inflection.

'If you would like to ride, you may join the party tomorrow. Surely you would love to join Uncle Herbert's ride. We have mounts aplenty, of that I am sure.'

Geraldine turned back to the window. 'Thank you. That might be rather pleasant.' It was all she could say. Perhaps a ride would set her thinking right. But was she giving in? Would riding properly, side-saddle, behind her uncle and two of his managers, and perhaps a female guest, sedately all over Gallantrae, put her mind off her misery?

CHAPTER EIGHT

In which a wedding takes place
and
Athena experiences a touch of envy

It was better than nothing. Geraldine sat on a docile mount and followed the riding party at a sedate pace, enjoying the countryside. Better than nothing; but how could she stop wishing for a more sprightly horse, a man's saddle, and a companion who urged her on, taking jumps and galloping along at a fearless rate?

She had not seen Mary Mark for some time, being lodged at Gallantrae. It was doubtful whether, as a married woman, she would be left to her own resources and ride daily. She had no idea—with little or no preparation or advice from her distracted mother, Lady Croukerne—what awaited her after the wedding. But she was sure of one thing; she would learn all she could about running the estate, which would keep her occupied and interested. Uncle Herbert was right. It would also give her opportunity to ride more, contrary to what everyone thought a married woman should do.

Even that day, she had been entreated not to join the ride. 'You might fall and break a leg, and what will we do about the wedding?'

Geraldine had been thrown by frisky or spooked mounts a number of times, but never told her mother, or her aunt, that her expedient was to roll on the ground, stand up, and get back into the saddle. Lady Croukerne would have been horrified.

But it was true that Geraldine was preoccupied about the wedding. It was daunting, and nothing in her experience could prepare her. She was astonished to receive a note at breakfast. Angus announced, in a few terse words, that they would be travelling to Italy not long after they wed.

Well, perhaps she would find occasion to ride in the countryside there. There was a grouping of paintings at Denisthorn Hall that she hardly gave mind to, but to which she would return now for a good look. They were paintings bought by her parents when on their grand tour of Europe, and pictured favourite locations in Italy where they had stopped and acquired souvenirs of their visit in the form of watercolours.

They were beautiful pictures, romantically portrayed, so she took heart in the opportunity to broaden her horizons in such lovely surroundings. She thought of exploring ruins, visiting famous monuments, and delighting in exceptional Mediterranean gardens.

'How exciting for you, my dear.' Her aunt was more delighted with the news than Geraldine. She had only been to Paris with the family as a child, travelling with two maids, a nanny, and a valet. An Italian tour with only her future husband was something that would have to unfold its mysteries to her as they travelled.

> *Sir Wilfred Harling has a fully-staffed house there, and is offering it to me for two months this year. We shall take him up on it, dear Geraldine, and see the sights before resuming our busy lives in*

England.

At any other time in her life, Geraldine would have been thrilled. Now, so unsure of her situation, and so full of the desire to pore over maps and books, doubts pushed their way into head and heart. 'I suppose so, Aunt Margery.' She had read the paragraph at table, and both her aunt and Sir Herbert wished her a pleasant sojourn in Italy later that year.

'You will need an appropriate travelling wardrobe. Light dresses, straw hats, muslin scarves, white gloves! I can help you with decisions in that regard.' Lady Margery raised an eyebrow, knowing her niece's lack of style. She understood Geraldine's mind did not often dwell on fashion, but appearing at breakfast as she did, in a day dress that was a good four years behind the current fashion, was enough to make the older woman take control where she could. How could a niece of hers travel to foreign parts looking like something out of an old journal? How could her sister, Lady Edwina Croukerne, allow her daughters to roam free in society wearing ensembles and accessories that were in such poor taste?

The big day arrived and ended, leaving everyone exhausted and not a little perplexed. A number of things worried Lord Croukerne. Although he duly walked his daughter up the aisle, leaving his hound with a groom, he felt—and looked, to all who watched—decidedly uncomfortable in his wheelchair, with Thorn his valet discreetly pushing him along.

'It was thoroughly modern of you, Edwina, to allow

your husband to wheel Geraldine to the altar!' One observer was heard to exclaim to Lady Croukerne, who appeared a little confused, emotional, or distracted throughout. Towards the end, when people were departing after dining, dancing, and partaking of the visually and palatably sensational wedding cake, she was heard to remark to Geraldine. 'I am so glad your little brother could see you dancing in your wedding gown, my dear.'

Startled and not a little worried, Geraldine decided to ignore her mother's remark, resolving to enjoy all that ensued after the wedding, despite misgivings about Angus, who either showered her with contrived phrases—which she sometimes found trite—or ignored her for hours at a time.

Gown, cake, dinner and music were a resounding success. All guests exclaimed at the novelty of a round flat cake, and swooned over the petits fours. The musicians were superlative, and played almost without a break.

Lady Athena, back home from London for the occasion, found it in her heart to leave the limelight to her younger sister. In the company of her friend Miss Blockley, she showed off new frocks bought in London, regaled little knots of people with social gossip, and generally kept out of Geraldine's way. She spent a lot of time getting to know the Croukerne's distant cousins, some of whom travelled from Manchester and Scotland, and were staying at Denisthorn. She made it quite plain to Lady Croukerne that she feared the wedding celebration might be a bit old-fashioned, but was pleased to note it surpassed her expectations.

'Well, my mother has surpassed herself,' she observed to Miss Blockley.

'She does have an enviable housekeeper.'

Athena nodded and adjusted her gloves. 'Indeed—something every wife and mother needs. I intend finding someone just as good as Mrs Beste.'

'You need to be married first, Athena, and to establish your own household.'

'Geraldine has it all set up for her. Moving in at Denisthorn, due to Papa's infirmity, seems to have turned out to be a silver lining for her.'

Her friend looked sideways at her and fluttered a fan. 'I heard her say how much she is learning through mere perusal of the ledgers, reports, and account books. Why, I do think I detect a touch of envy, my dear friend.'

'Nothing of the sort! When I get established—something which I do not foresee to be far into the future—I shall make sure my rich husband puts everything at my disposal for a grand household, complete with a full complement of capable staff.' She looked across the room at her sister, who seemed to float about on a cloud of muslin and white Belgian lace.

'The queen started something, this matter of having a white wedding dress is sure to become more than just a fashion.'

'No! Give it a few years, and people will forget. Honestly, a white wedding dress is the height of impracticability. Where would one wear it afterwards? With her presentation at court behind her, any young woman would see no use for such a gown.' Athena looked at her sister in her frothy dress and frowned.

'I think it glorious, even if a bit of a waste.'

Geraldine hoped that now the wedding was over, she and her sister might settle into some sort of cordial interaction, but she was too weary to even contemplate measures or solutions that day.

What remained was to retire to the suite upstairs and rest after a somewhat demanding day, when not a single opportunity to take a breath was made available. To Geraldine's mind, too much ado was made among too many guests on too long an event.

'There were people there I hardly knew, and faces I have never before seen!'

'You had never met my colleagues, nor my friends from university, nor my distant cousin from South Africa,' Angus replied.

They were to spend their first night at Gallantrae, and return to Denisthorn the following day. There were no obvious signs that he might be happy, or proud, or enthusiastic about the future. Her new husband disappeared to his dressing room with his valet, promising to join Geraldine in twenty minutes.

It was a half-hour during which she quaked inside. She had only the vaguest concept of what a wedding night might consist of, and she had asked Fairley, herself not a deep fount of information, never having been married.

'I read in a ladies' journal, my lady, that one must clear the mind and use fortitude, forbearance and trust.'

Such abstract information, without a physical addendum of advice, was not useful to Geraldine, to whom 'clearing the mind' meant thinking of something else besides what daunted her. Thinking of horses, thinking of home, thinking of Mary Mark.

She thought of the queen, who produced—and so seemingly easily—a battery of children, and who was so enamoured of her Prince Consort. Surely if Victoria Regina could do it, she could do no less. But the thought of a battery of children scared her, and the advances of an enamoured man were even less palatable. She continued to quake inside.

Even her grandmother had been useless, coming through with the advice of detachment. 'Any sensible woman would do well to detach herself mentally from her marital obligations, my dear Geraldine. There are expedients. A fortifying nightcap is one, and also the consolation that men are easily satisfied, and rapidly fall asleep once they have found their goal. That's all it is, a goal. Let your husband find his goal easily, and it is over before it has begun.'

'Is that right?'

'You will see,' the dowager marchioness said, and raised both eyebrows cryptically.

Did the advice help her now? She was afraid it did not.

'I cannot wait to get back to Denisthorn, Cousin Angus,' she said to him plainly when he returned, without his valet. Fairley had left her a few minutes before, and they were alone.

'Well, it's to bed, I suppose,' he said. 'We'll be at Denisthorn Hall soon enough.'

'To take up a new life.' She tried to be bright. 'I cannot wait to go over the entire estate by your side.'

'Is that a fact?' He kissed her on the cheek and

climbed into bed without waiting for her to get in first. *Forbearance*, she remembered. Gathering her nightgown skirt around her, she arranged herself in a pose; what she considered a man might consider pretty. *Let him find his goal.* Taking a deep breath, she looked round at Angus.

He was already fast asleep.

Lord and Lady Croukerne looked Geraldine up and down on her return to Denisthorn. They stood on the forecourt with most of the staff lined up, since it was their entrance as the future holders of the seat.

'You do not look much changed,' her mother said, looking her hard in the face, searching her eyes.

'Perhaps it is because I am not.' In her heart, she felt that she would never become her sister, which was what she thought her mother meant.

In fact, it was Mrs Jones, the cook, who let her know what her parents—and indeed everyone in the house—was looking for.

'Of course they look you up and down, my dear Miss Gera.' It was her name for Lady Geraldine since childhood. 'They are looking to see you changed into a married woman.'

'I am married.'

'In the physical sense, my dear. That you have been *known* by a man.' If it was possible for Mrs Jones to blush, she would have.

Geraldine did not divulge the fact to her what happened the previous night. She did not say Angus had fallen into a deep sleep the instant his head touched the pillow, probably from too much drink and too much dancing at his own wedding. She did not say that he was up and out of bed when she woke, to find he had joined Sir Herbert on a ride.

They met at the breakfast table, where her aunt did look her up and down, probably to find no change. 'You are down to breakfast, dear. Married women do not need to do that.'

Perhaps she was wrong. Perhaps she was not expected to fulfil wifely duties on the first night. Perhaps she needed advice from someone who knew about these things, like a doctor.

She thought better of going to a man with her questions, and tapped on the closed door of the housekeeper's office. 'Mrs Beste—may I have a moment?'

They had a brief conversation, preceded by a shy and awkward pause during which Geraldine told of her ambition of understanding how Denisthorn estate was run.

After Mrs Beste divested herself of her astonished expression at the young woman's question, which was the only reason she was there, Geraldine left her office clutching to her chest—lest someone read its title—a little book.

CHAPTER NINE

In which Lady Athena receives a visitor
and
London is crowded with army officers

Lord Croukerne did not relish travelling to London often, because his infirmity. The hated wheelchair put a dampening feeling on something he used to love doing. But a peer in the House of Lords had obligations to fulfil, so with perseverance and a good valet, he endeavoured to take the train. Arriving rather tired, after an uncomfortable ride from the station in the brougham, he was pleased that the house was open, and that Athena was firmly settled with her companion in the fine residence.

Cosmo the hound was quickly taken down to the service yard for a feed, and then returned by his master's side.

Maud Blockley was enjoying her long stay in the bustling city, participating in as many events and celebrations to which she could obtain invitations, and she and Athena were frequently to be seen at the assembly rooms.

It was at a musical gathering, planned to introduce a new string ensemble to London, at which the two young ladies—never too far from each other—found that a regiment was in town.

'The Royal Lancers are here, how exciting!'

'They do look smart in their red and blues.' She watched a group of young army officers standing near the end windows. 'They must be on their way to India from Ireland.'

'Oh, Athena—how is it that you are privy to the movements of Her Majesty's armies?' She cocked her head at her friend. 'I'm sure Queen Victoria herself is not as adjourned as you are. Tell me your secret!'

'It's no secret. I pay attention to what my father says at table, simply to derive information suitable for conversation. I used to find good conversation was my weakness, and was scolded several times by Aunt Margery.'

'You did say she thinks you speak in monosyllables!'

'Well, not any more, if I can help it. And, for your information, all regiment movements are announced in the daily papers. I take note of those, and sometimes prefer it to this social whirl.' She did sincerely and silently hope her social graces would improve, for there was no other way to make a good match.

'You read the men's papers!'

'I believe they are written for anyone willing to read them.'

The arch reply was taken in good grace by her friend, who was accustomed to her ripostes. 'Do you remember Lady Verney?' she asked.

'Yes, I do. Her third daughter has just been married. An excellent match, I hear.' She sighed. 'A good match. I heard they have been installed at *Cromby*

Castle.'

Miss Blockley detected envy in her tone, but said nothing. 'Well, Lady Verney is coming our way, with four Lancers in tow!'

'Oh dear, another set of introductions. We shall never remember any of the officer's names.'

Captain Walter Phisgrove was memorable to Miss Blockley, and not only for his handsome looks. His family name and reputation were unimpeachable. He towered above the others, taking the hand of each young lady in turn, and quite eclipsed the other officers.

'Did you see his hair?' She whispered to Athena.

'Whose?'

'Captain Phisgrove's!'

Athena smirked. 'His head is so high above all others it's a wonder we can see his chin.'

'Oh, Athena! I despair of your attitude. If you desire to make ...'

'Of course! Of course I desire to make myself a splendid match. But young soldiers—young men—like Captain Phisgrove are tiresome. Dull. They have little to say for themselves.'

'What are you interested in, then, Athena? Because I fail to see how you think.'

'Not guns, horses, travel, battles. Certainly not. That is all they talk about.'

Miss Blockley watched Captain Phisgrove, who was now circling the room, while she listened to her friend. She watched him closely as he spoke, tilted his head, gazed around the room, and shook hands. 'Look at him—he does it all so gracefully.'

'I have no interest in grace, Maud. Stare at him all

you like, but it will change neither his age, nor his interests, nor the fact that he stands a good two feet above all of us.'

Maud Blockley shook her head. 'There is a certain charm in young men. Such energy, such enthusiasm. It's what I think, at any rate. And look, Captain Phisgrove has gone all around the room, and I do believe he is coming our way again.'

'The music will start soon.'

'Surely we can get a sentence in before it does.' Miss Blockley's smile dulled a little when she saw the captain walk up to Athena.

'Lady Athena, I do think ...'

'Excuse me, Captain. I'm afraid I have been summoned. I mean, I am required elsewhere.' Athena bobbed a cursory curtsey and hurried away, leaving the captain and Miss Blockley facing each other, a touch embarrassed by Athena's hasty departure.

Simpson tidied away ribbons, stockings, and what she felt were a thousand pins. Sticking them into the new pincushion on the dressing table, she hunted for more. It would not do to leave one hidden in the rug, and risk Lady Athena finding it with a toe.

She folded two stoles, paired shoes and slippers to remove to the dressing room, and looked around the room. Lady Athena's bedroom in this London house was much smaller than the one at Denisthorn, but seemed somehow more elegant and modern. Lord Croukerne had had the London house redone just before his accident, at some expense, and if it were not for his present disability, would have opened it to friends and acquaintances often. With his daughter in the city, there would have been a veritable calendar of soirees, parties and luncheons, but being in a wheelchair slowed him down, tired him, made him less eager to entertain or hold social events.

Simpson was sorry for Lord Croukerne, but was not sorry social events were less numerous than they could have been. Being kept busy was fine in her opinion, but getting too tired every day was not anything she could enjoy. She was getting used to spending time reading, and in her time off in London, appreciated a brisk walk every afternoon. There were so many other ladies' maids, nannies and governesses in the nearby park at that time that she was never short of people to converse with. There was nothing she liked better than a spot of news, which any other person might have termed gossip. It gave her an understanding of what Lady Athena spoke about, and perhaps knowledge of society movements before her mistress, which gave her the occasional shiver of pleasure. The occasional feeling of being ahead of the rest of the household. She had just learned the previous day, for example, that Mr Phineas Gow was in town.

'Now that should lead to something interesting,' she said to her reflection as she wound a few hairs off Lady Athena's brush for the waste basket. Knowing she would never be married herself, since it was now too late and she was starting to be valued as a good lady's maid, she accepted that she would enjoy married life by proxy, through her mistress. But Lady Athena had to find a match first.

In the day sitting room, it was quieter than usual.

'Papa does not even take pleasure in a game of cards any longer, or to linger after dinner with the gentlemen. He excuses himself early and takes to his rooms.' Athena put down the small book of poems she was given as a gift.

'It must be hard.' Miss Purl, who was not enjoying London as much as she had anticipated, looked up from her crewel work. Being a companion and chaperone was full of opportunity, of course. She listened to good music, ate good food, witnessed the exciting fashions of the season, and watched young people turn into the influential personages of the future. But personally, it all held little change. She gave required responses, and strove to appear calm and unruffled, but dependable.

'He realizes less than Mama, perhaps, how important it is for me.'

'You were invited to Sir Michael's this evening.'

'I let Maud go in the company of Mrs Fox and Lady Eveline. I could not bear to converse with another young officer. Not after last night.'

Miss Purl smiled. 'I hear they have taken over the city. London is painted red and blue.'

'Red and blue?'

'Uniforms, Lady Athena.'

'Ah, I see. I do not care in the least. I am ...' she twirled a pencil. 'I am preparing a list of guests for a dinner. And I'll discuss it with the housekeeper tomorrow, and then with Papa. Some solid conversation at a dinner table with some older gentlemen will be just the ticket.'

Miss Purl looked up again, her lips tight. The words *Some wealthier gentlemen* rolled through her mind. 'Yes. That ought to be more suitable, Lady Athena.' She tittered and went on with her needle. 'When do you plan to have it?'

'A fortnight from tomorrow. I hear some important gentlemen from Scotland are in town to see to some banking concerns.'

'Oh! Does that include Lady Geraldine's husband, Mr Angus Crownrigg?'

'It might, but I was not thinking of him, although it might be an oversight not to include him in the party.' She quickly wrote *Angus Crownrigg* on the list.

The gentleman she had in mind was a great deal older than her sister's new husband. And a great deal less handsome, but she was not to be swayed by handsomeness, or youth, or the glib things that spouted from the mouths of young men. They had less sense than they had energy, and their predatory looks put her off.

'Predatory,' she said under her breath.

'I beg your pardon?'

'I was just mouthing words to myself, Miss Purl. I did not mean to disturb you.'

'No disturbance.' But the companion had heard the word, which she usually associated with animals, such as eagles, hawks, lions and hyenas. 'Shall we be going to the zoological gardens, do you think?'

'Capital idea—I have heard they are now undertaking to show off the animals as they might appear in their natural habitats.'

'Natural habitats?'

'They allow them to run in the open, rather than in cages.'

'Oh! Is it at all safe?'

Athena smiled. 'It is all well-regulated, from what I read, with boundaries and fences. Enclosures, I think the word used is. I saw it in the paper.'

'I'm sure it is quite amusing to Lord Croukerne that you take a turn at the papers after he has risen from the library.'

'He has a good chuckle, I'm sure, Miss Purl. As do you. But I am ultimately better informed than most of the ladies at the assembly rooms.' It was Athena's turn to chuckle.

A footman entered bearing a tray full of calling cards.

Miss Purl looked and then lowered her eyes to her embroidery. She looked quite surprised to see so many cards.

Athena looked up at the footman. 'Well, thank you, Hayes. There were many callers this afternoon.'

'More than just a few,' the young man replied. 'And three did enquire after Miss Blockley. Officers, my lady.'

Athena shook her head. After the footman left the room, she shuffled through the cards and smiled. 'I did think that Captain Phisgrove would be showing interest, and yes—he has left his card.'

'Miss Blockley would do well to entertain the interest this year. Is she not a whole year older than you?' Miss Purl cut an end of cotton and placed it in a small envelope. *And about twice the weight.* They were words she could not say.

'Are you always so tidy, Miss Purl, placing

discarded cotton inside an old envelope?'

'I was taught tidiness by my nurse when I was little. She taught me basic stitches, and supervised my very first sampler. She also taught me observation, and how to detect the mood of a room on entering.'

'How interesting! So you have no doubt noted,' Athena said pointedly, 'how many cards were on this afternoon's salver.'

'I have indeed. And I do wish your friend the best this season. It is a hectic one, with two regiments in the city.'

'Yes, I did hear a cavalry was arriving as well.'

'Not something that would enhance your spirits.'

'No, Miss Purl. No—I am not in the least bit interested in the military.'

'I suppose the nobility, then.'

'Oh, I am avidly interested in business. The railways have opened up the entire country. Commerce and trade are booming. So many gentlemen are being industrious and successful ... and being knighted for it!'

'Knighted! For business?'

'By the queen. I am sure it is a practice that will continue. The Prince of Wales, who will eventually be our king, will no doubt continue to do it. I read that he is deeply interested in finance. In the economy, I think the words are. And in dealings with foreign countries. So business men are not only accruing wealth, but gaining gentility and social position. And there can be nothing wrong in that.'

'I have heard the prince is also interested in the theatre.'

Athena's brow creased with her frown. 'We must

not believe all we hear, Miss Purl. I know you infer hearsay bandied around about an actress.' Her lips drew a straight line.

The footman re-entered the room. 'Mr Phineas Gow and Mrs Elizabeth Gorman, my lady.'

There was nothing on Athena's face for Miss Purl to detect whether her young companion was pleased or not with the visit.

The gentleman inclined his head and took her hand. 'Lady Athena, we cannot stay long. I beg to introduce Mrs Elizabeth Gorman, who is leaving London today and said how delighted she would be to make your acquaintance.'

They smiled at each other, and Athena made a graceful arched wave with a hand to suggest they should be seated. 'I can ring for some tea.'

'Och, I doubt we have that much time, I'm afraid.' Mr Gow looked apologetic. 'This has to be brief, because I have a board meeting very shortly. I just wanted to ensure you know how pleased I am to see you in London.'

'It is a pleasure for me as well.' A pretty tilt of her head, and Athena's eyes met those of the gentleman who was said by her mother to be the ugliest she had ever set eyes on. 'Are you leaving by train, Mrs Gorman?' She addressed the newcomer, her voice not changing tenor in the least.

The conversation turned to the convenience of trains to Edinburgh, and how that means of conveyance had shortened travel times and seemed to have shrunken the United Kingdom.

In ten minutes, they were gone.

'That was a lightning visit, to be sure,' Miss Purl said, as the footman who showed the visitors out shut the door.

'But gratefully received. Since he is Cousin Angus's uncle, it cannot be a bad thing to make better acquaintance with Mr Gow.'

'Could it be that introducing Mrs Gorman was an excuse? Is she not the widow of that Mr Francis Gorman who was newly elected to parliament and then died suddenly?' Athena's companion stuck a needle into her pincushion, sighed, and sat back.

'Well—if it was an excuse, I am all the more grateful. It might mean he has every intention in the world of strengthening bonds in the family.'

'Or perhaps he is interested in Mrs Gorman, since I think he said he is a widower. Might he not want the family to make her acquaintance?'

Athena frowned for the second time in just a bit more than half an hour. She had not given that scenario any thought. It was a possibility.

'What do you think?' Miss Purl raised an eyebrow.

Athena drew a breath and placed a hand to her waist. She hoped Miss Purl would not detect her unease, which she could not entirely analyse herself. She hoped that on her return from London, her sister would not crow and swagger at her older sister being still without an offer.

Miss Purl required a response. 'In either case, it was a pleasure to see Mr Gow again.' Not betraying her thoughts in the least, she held in a sigh. She had hoped to see Mr Gow while he was in London from Scotland, but was not expecting him to introduce her to any new people in this way.

'An invitation or two might arise from this.'

'Oh, I do hope not, Miss Purl! I have enough invitations already to fill the mantelpiece.'

'I thought it was the reason we came to London for the season. How else could one hope to see and be seen?'

'Indeed.' Athena slumped back in her armchair. 'How else?'

CHAPTER TEN

In which a proposal is awaited
and
Angus Crownrigg makes his first married mistake

Miss Blockley picked up a pleat on her day dress and let it fall onto her lap again. She sat with Athena in the Belgrave house, in the larger sitting room, which had a dual aspect, but looked over the street. Through the sheer curtains, they could see—although not completely clearly—much movement and carriage traffic. Even some officers on horseback; red and blue jackets above head height passing to and fro. The animated street scene was enough to make the young women eager to be outdoors.

'I do not know why you insisted on staying indoors today, Maud.' Athena watched her friend play with the pleats on her skirt. 'I was so inclined to ask for the open carriage to take a turn in Hyde Park. There is so much activity today, out of doors.'

'And I do not know why I put on this dress today. My girl Sarah said it becomes me, and that it came fresh from being thoroughly cleaned, so I let her lay it out, but this colour now seems a bit too wan for company.' She looked up, hoping her companion would not detect the mistake she made.

Athena widened her eyes. 'Ah! For company! You are expecting some caller. That would explain your reluctance to go out, and your intense interior monologue about dress colour!'

She had hardly said the last word when a footman opened the door. 'Captain Walter Phisgrove and Captain Ian MacTavish of the Royal Lancers are here, Lady Athena.'

The announcement was enough to make Athena blink hard, and Miss Blockley to simper prettily. Her broad cheeks and heightened colour meant she was fully expecting this call.

'Tea, I think, Hayes.' Athena spoke to the footman, then turned to the young officers. 'You are paying visits on such a sunny day, which is unusual, Captain Phisgrove, Captain MacTavish. It is not our usual day for being at home.'

'It is a pleasant duty, Lady Athena. And we thought we would take a risk and beg your indulgence.'

'Duty! My, how old-fashioned!' She waved a hand to indicate the men could be seated. With their hats under their arms and standing, they seemed to fill the room to the ceiling.

'We are awaiting deployment, Miss Blockley. And before we are called, a visit is called for. I intend to make the journey to Worcestershire, you see. I am sure the train goes as far as Cheltenham.'

'Yes, of course it does—what takes you to the country, Captain?' Athena was curious, but she could see that Miss Blockley was privy to the reason for Captain Phisgrove's journey. A realization showed its gleam on her face. 'Ah! I *see*.'

The other young man had not spoken a word since arrival. It was plain he was there to make up the numbers.

Athena looked at him expectantly. 'And you, Captain MacTavish. Will you be making the trip as well?'

'Garrison duties keep me in London until the regiment moves, Lady Athena. Walter will be travelling on his own.'

No more was said about the journey, and when tea was brought in on a trolley, talk centred around the weather. There was also mention of a play, to be performed at the new theatre.

'It will be a crowded affair, because the Prince of Wales will be there, and any event at a new theatre is sure to draw vast crowds.'

'Can you imagine the line of carriages? Perhaps I should prefer to see the new place when the novelty has worn a little.'

When the officers left, Athena stood, flounced her skirts and turned to her friend. 'You do realize why Captain Phisgrove is journeying to the country, don't you? He is ...'

'He intends to make it a quick thing. He's going to ...'

'... to talk to ...'

'To talk to Papa, yes!' Maud Blockley held a hand to her throat, her apple cheeks bright, her lips pursed in delight.

'I must say, Maud. Is this not outrageously rapid? Why, you have only met Captain Phisgrove a couple of times. Why, you could not count your encounters on more than one hand! And he is speaking to your father, to ask for your hand.'

Miss Blockley blushed. 'One encounter would have

been enough. We seem to get along rather well. Walter and I spoke. I mean, we conversed at length on more than two occasions, and he has said that he ... '

'*Walter and I!*' Athena heaved a puff of indignation. 'How quickly we abandon civility and propriety.'

'Oh, Athena, please don't be upset.'

Athena's face was a picture of confusion. 'There will be no one left at all. I shall be the only one left. The shelf! I shall be on the shelf, the only unmarried woman of my age *anywhere*.'

It was very quiet at Denisthorn. Lord Croukerne was in London, as was Lady Athena. Although Geraldine and Angus had departed for Italy, Lady Edwina was constantly startled when someone opened the door, expecting one or the other of her daughters to appear.

'I do believe this is the quietest it has ever been at Denisthorn,' she said to Mrs Beste, as they discussed yet another week's menus.

'With the young ladies gone, my lady, we are all in train of cleaning, reorganizing and putting things to rights, both downstairs and in the house. There is more to do in Lady Geraldine's new suite.' The housekeeper, prim and straight, was nothing if not efficient and exact. 'We do want everything to be shipshape for her return.'

But Lady Croukerne was still daydreaming. 'Nanny should allow the little baron to run around a bit more freely. It is such a delight to see him run past my window with his hoop!'

The housekeeper said nothing. She was well aware, from talk below stairs, that all servants had noticed, and discussed, the turn for the illusory their mistress had taken.

'He is growing out of his jackets. We must get someone to let them out for him. Simpson, perhaps.'

'Simpson is in London with Lady Athena, my lady.'

'Of course she is. How forgetful of me. Lady Geraldine, then, will be coming to sit with me soon, and perhaps read me a chapter out of *The Mayor of Casterbridge*. Such an interesting novel.'

'Lady Geraldine and Mr Crownrigg are on their travels in Italy, my lady.'

'Oh! How will I ever keep up with all the family's comings and goings?'

'Is Lady Margery not due for tea this afternoon? She should be able to remind you of the whereabouts of everyone.' In a reassuring tone, Mrs Beste tried to put Lady Croukerne's mind at rest. She was glad of the fact her mistress's sister lived within a reasonable distance. Close enough to make regular visits to keep Lady Croukerne abreast of things and of sound enough mind.

Below stairs, three maids took advantage of Mrs Beste's absence from the servants' hall to giggle and gossip about the housekeeper's frequent visits to the village.

'Mr Pillow is not the most handsome of men.'

'Ha ha—nor the most flushed with silver!'

'I'd say that copper coins are the most he would run to.'

'Oh no, Maisie. He's a shopkeeper, and they run into a fair number of sixpences and shillings, I do suppose. Just think of the amounts of money crossing that counter. Changing hands, as it were.'

'*As it were*! Be careful, or you'll turn into a lady with that language, Hattie!'

'Shan't be surprised to hear Mr Pillow has salted away a great deal in florins and half crowns, never mind sixpences. But Mrs Beste would do well to find out, to make certain, afore she spends too much time supping tea with him at the blue tearoom!'

'Is that what you do when you set eyes on a young man, Hattie?'

'My time is not come. I'm fifteen. In a year or so, I shall set eyes on someone who can afford a decent cottage, with a decent wage, and keep us in a decent situation.'

'How decent!'

They laughed together, but heard the creak of the baize door and scattered, two to the kitchen, and one to make a great pretence of sweeping out the hall fireplace.

'What are you doing there at this time of day, Hattie? That's a chore best left for the early morning. Let the thing settle, girl. And I'd better talk to Mr Herring about getting one of the boys to oil the hinges on the baize door. The creaks are loud enough to be heard all the way down to the mirror lake!'

'Are they, Mrs Beste?'

''You know they are, Hattie, for you took up this silly sweeping when you heard I was coming down.'

Venice was nothing like its illustration watercolour hanging in Lord Croukerne's library. Geraldine was dismayed to arrive at a station that seemed to be still in construction, on a site where an old church was not yet completely demolished. It was difficult to step down onto the makeshift wooden platform. Builders, hawkers, porters, messengers and everyone else seemed to shout at the tops of their voices even in normal conversation. Hammering, digging and the creaking of carthorse harnesses, even the grinding of wooden wheels upon uneven ground, added to the cacophony.

'My goodness, Angus, this is so confusing. We should have arrived by steamship. We should have listened to Papa.'

But Geraldine's husband was distracted, pointing to this bridge and that and trying to say sentences in Italian, which were met by much laughter. He turned to her. 'Steamship? No, no, my dear. Lord Harling was quite adamant that the new railway station would do perfectly well, and look—here we are.'

Overhead, enormous flights of birds wove in swarms, and a heavy layer of cloud rendered everything grey, even the much-renowned waters of the lagoon, which shimmered towards their eyes a silvery glimmer, with streaks that were green rather than blue. Church bells rang in the distance, as if to welcome her, her alone, for no one else seemed to notice them above the din.

'I do believe, Geraldine, that we must now take a gondola.' Angus looked around, perplexed.

'A gondola! But they are so small. Did you not let Lord Harling know the day of our arrival?'

'Lord Harling is in London. The House of Lords is sitting.'

Geraldine uttered a quiet exclamation. She inhaled, catching the aroma of the water. 'So how are we to reach his palace?' She wondered whether they would ever get clear of the noise. She also wondered whether their luggage would reach the destination. All the bags and her precious box had been carted off on a rig pulled along by three barefoot boys. She stood and looked across a stretch of water over which a crowded bridge, which seemed to be made only of wood, did not seem to be the means she would prefer to use to cross the water.

'Geraldine, my dear, it seems we must take a ...' Angus was interrupted by an older man with extremely white hair.

'I take you, signore.'

'You take me?' Angus seemed nonplussed.

But Geraldine was glad to hear words in English, no matter how puzzling. 'Will you take us to Palazzo Grimani?'

'Sì, Sì!' He nodded yes, turned, and started to walk away, leaving Geraldine and Angus no choice but to follow him out of the crowd and further away from the deafening sounds outside the station.

'Has Lord Harling sent you?'

In barely decipherable English, the little old man said that no, he was not Lord Harling.

'Of course you are not!'

'But has he sent you to meet us?'

'I take you.' He said it twice or three times more, and led them to some slippery steps in front of another church. He bowed and indicated a large rowing boat, where their luggage lay.

Heaving a sigh of relief to see her box, Geraldine gave her hand to a waiting oarsman and stepped onto the tilting boards of the boat. If she had known, if she had not thought that they would be arriving at a splendid palace, she would have worn a riding habit as a travelling outfit, and made herself a bit more comfortable and confident.

When Angus got on board, the vessel tilted alarmingly, and Geraldine nearly uttered a scream.

'If we get to Palazzo Grimani without incident, it will be the surprise of my life, Geraldine.'

'Oh, please do not say that, Cousin Angus.'

'I have no idea what these coins are worth. I have already given the old man and the boatman money, and they will either take me for a fool, or a spendthrift.'

'They looked to me like Austrian money.'

'Well, Emperor Franz Joseph was on the florin. Do you think their florin is much like ours?'

Geraldine glared at her new husband. 'Did you give them florins? They will certainly think you are unwise.'

'A fool, I know.' Angus smiled. Then he pointed. 'Look, that is St Mark's, but it looks to me that we are going further.'

Angus hailed forward to the old man with a question. 'Didn't we say Palazzo Grimani, my man? I thought it was up the Grand Canal.'

'*Canale Grande*,' the man said through a mouth of broken teeth. He pointed.

'We're heading away from there.'

'*Canale Grande*,' he said again, and nodded.

They proceeded slowly, for they had hit the current entering the canal from the lagoon. The boat tipped this way and that, with little choppy waves hitting it broadside. Geraldine felt slightly unwell, and Angus turned pale.

But it was not long before they came alongside a wharf, and the old man bade them to disembark. The man who met them with another handcart seemed—if possible—even older than the one who helped Geraldine off, and then Angus. They regained balance, and adjusted to the breeze coming off the water.

'I should have brought Fairley.' Geraldine felt cut off from all that was safe and sensible. 'Fairley would have been of assistance in all this. She is so practical.' But they had been told that the palace was fully staffed, and they would be taken care of very well.

When at last they reached an arched doorway, after a circuitous route on foot along narrow alleys, the old man stopped.

'Is this Palazzo Grimani?' Geraldine was footsore and anxious.

The man turned and pointed. 'Is that.'

They regarded a narrow portal flanked by ornate columns.

'So what's this?'

'Is Harling 'ouse, signora.'

The door was thrown open by a woman in an apron. '*Ah, benvenuti! Signore e signora* Crownrigg.' She pronounced each syllable clearly. 'Much welcome, much welcome.'

They were relieved, and at the same time puzzled by the house. 'We thought we were to stay at Palazzo Grimani.'

The woman laughed. 'Is empty. Is a ruin. Is old like museum. No one stay there.' She pointed at the hallway behind her. 'You stay at Casa 'Arling, is *close to* Palazzo Grimani.'

Angus paid the old man with more florins, and the door was shut. Everything went quiet quite suddenly, which was such a relief to Geraldine she raised hands to her ears.

'I shall leave you to settle things, my dear.' Angus looked at her, a small frown creasing his forehead.

'You can't leave me! I should not know what to say, what to do!'

'And we shall meet again at dinner, perhaps.'

'Perhaps! Angus, please see reason. I don't know these people. I don't know that our accommodations will be what we expect.'

'Of course they will be. Lord Harling would hardly strand us in inferior lodgings.' With that, Angus let himself out of the door—which they were to discover was a back door—and disappeared.

Shown up a shallow stair case to a floor with exceedingly high ceilings, Geraldine found the woman, Tonietta, to be obliging and gentle. Her rooms were furnished in florid taste, but appropriate and quite clean.

'Will you be my maid, Tonietta?'

The girl tilted her head.

'Who will look after me?'

The girl laughed. 'Mamma will soon come. She buy provision. For *cena*. She look after you good.'

A few questions revealed that *cena* meant dinner, which boded well.

Geraldine divested herself of her travelling clothes as soon as her box was brought up. Resting in an ornate gilt armchair in a dressing robe, she recovered somewhat, and lectured herself in practicality. She had to be resourceful and wise, happy and capable if she was to enjoy her honeymoon. If she was to enjoy anything. She was the adventurous one in the family, the most intrepid. Expecting to find everything as she would in England was at the very least unimaginative. It was what the trip was all about—discovery, adventure, new knowledge. She was known for her spirit of adventure, her ability to seize opportunities.

'I shall strive to enjoy every step. I must learn independence, and self-worth.'

She repeated the word *cena* to herself, feeling rather hungry, since no refreshment was offered on arrival. She discovered a decanter of what looked like wine and an enormous bunch of grapes on a side table. She helped herself to some and felt better. She supposed it was ridiculous to expect tea in a country like Italy. She would wait for dinner, and see what was being prepared for them.

As it happened, she dined alone. Angus did not return, and Tonietta and her mother, Mamma Clara, did not wait. They served her in a small dining room full of little angel statues on plinths, which at any other time might have seemed delightful. The fact Angus did not make an appearance was unsettling. It was something Geraldine found hard to understand.

He left her to wonder at the dishes all on her own. She ate what she thought was a fish course, and then a piece of pie, filled with some kind of fowl, and then a dish of fried vegetables, and a cheese course. Although unusual, it was more than just edible, and if it were not for Angus's absence, would have been a lot more enjoyable.

She did not see him before breakfast the next day.

CHAPTER ELEVEN

In which Lady Geraldine realizes something important
and
Milly Fairley realizes the benefits of her new position

Milly Fairley pulled back the curtains in her mistress's bedroom at Denisthorn, noting the weather had cleared and it would be a sunny day, perfect for drying stockings and gathering some flowers for tray posies. The garden boy was supposed to bring in the flowers the gardeners sheaved up for him, and a kitchen maid was meant to make up the tray posies in the scullery, but Fairley needed something appealing in her day. She needed to fill the empty days until her mistress's return with something. Something pretty.

The other maids would exclaim if she said anything of the sort to them, because they thought her days were made up of pretty things, but the truth was that she was easily bored by her daily tasks. Tidying, folding, brushing hair, sorting out pins, putting away and laying out frocks and gowns, and making sure all jewellery was accounted for, might be engagement with many pretty things, but it was repetitive and monotonous. Besides, not having many pretty things of her own put her in a daily position of some envy. Why could she not have a diamond brooch? Why would she never own a string of pearls? Why was she restricted to one straw hat and one felt hat when she had to care for so many different hats and bonnets?

The dress she wore to church on Sundays was a hand-me-down, altered to fit. Lady Geraldine had looked at it, laid out on her bed. 'I'll wear this today for the last time, Fairley. Then please take it. You can take it up, or take it in, or add something to the bodice, and wear it yourself.'

'Thank you so much, my lady.' She had felt grateful at the time. After all, wearing a light blue Indian cotton dress with daisies printed all over was a real change from the heavy drill dress she usually wore to church, but after a few Sundays the novelty had worn off, and when she looked in her small grainy mirror she knew she would never be much more than a maid in discarded ladies' clothing.

She said so much to a housemaid in the servants' hall at lunch, only to be overheard by Mrs Beste. The housekeeper beckoned a finger at her and she was summoned to her office.

If this was to be a scolding, Fairley knew to bow her head and take it. Answering back was not received well by the housekeeper and the butler at Denisthorn, who determined what happened and how the world ran behind and below the baize door. She needed this position, and wanted to keep it, despite her occasional unhappiness.

'Milly Fairley, my girl, I know why you are feeling this way.' Mrs Beste's voice was kind as she closed the door for privacy.

'You do?'

'Come and sit by me.' Mrs Beste did not go round

behind her desk, but pulled two chairs together. 'I know you would have liked to travel to Italy with Lady Geraldine, but they are being looked after by Lord Harling's staff while she and Mr Crownrigg are in Venice.'

'I wasn't wanted,' the girl said. 'I know.'

'You are not *needed*, and there's a difference. Mr Crownrigg too is travelling without a valet.'

'It would never have happened some years ago. Why are things changing so much?'

'Things always change, my girl. Now, I'm sure Lady Geraldine misses you sorely, especially now that she is married and needs a sympathetic ear.'

'Do you suppose? Not wanted ... not needed. There's a difference?'

'Of course there is. It won't be long before they return, and much at Denisthorn will return to normal. Well, as normal as can be with Mr Crownrigg living here permanently.'

'I like doing the flowers in the morning. Will I still be able to do that?'

'You'll have a lot more to do. But yes, of course— do the tray posies. I've noticed you make rather pretty ones. And do make sure the newly-appointed rooms are perfect for their arrival. There is Lady Geraldine's bedroom, dressing room, and bathroom, all looking new and nicely done up. Ah—I remember when there were no bathrooms, just one in each corridor. We had to run up and down with hot water jugs. It's so much easier now, with a boiler that's plumbed to taps.' Mrs Beste snapped out of her thoughts. 'And there is talk of opening up the empty storey. That will involve much work. Ah, where was I? Yes. And Cromer, Mr Crownrigg's man, will see to his rooms. Have you been upstairs to have a look?'

'I have been keeping Lady Geraldine's old room clean and tidy.'

'That room will now be converted to a guest room. I'm sure Lady Croukerne will give it a name. You're to see that all the young lady's ... I'm sorry, I keep forgetting she is married now.' Mrs Beste smiled behind a hand. 'She will still be Lady Geraldine to us at home. In society, she will be known as Lady Crownrigg. You're to see that all Lady Geraldine's things are moved and placed in appropriate places in the new rooms, as close as possible to her old ways.'

'Which rooms are they?' Fairley was glad she had an important job to do in her mistress's absence. She was also glad that in comparison to Simpson, Lady Athena's maid, who was older in years, she had a superior station, as the maid of a married woman who would one day be mistress of Denisthorn. She had a lot to be grateful for. 'How much longer before they return?'

'The back corridor is where they will be. That means close to half of the ladies' corridor has been taken over for them. The end ones with the connecting door.'

'Connecting door, I see.'

'They are married, Milly.'

'I keep forgetting.'

'Yes, we both forget, don't we? Ah—and there's a sitting room for Lady Geraldine now, which used to be one of the front bedrooms. See that Maisie puts that to rights, and fill it with flowers for her return. So many changes. It's going to take some getting used to.'

Fairley tiptoed her way to the new rooms, and had a look around. Then she went down to the servants' hall to mend some of her own stockings, and to listen to Peter Formby tinkling on the piano.

Meanwhile, in Venice, Geraldine was missing her lady's maid sorely. Mamma Clara did not know how to look after an English lady, had no notion of modern hair fashion, did not see the difference between a day frock and an evening dress, and would lay out diamond jewellery in the morning.

'No diamonds before dusk, Mamma Clara.'

'*Daask*?'

'Six o'clock. No diamonds in daylight.'

'*Perchè*?'

'*Why*? I don't know why—it's just vulgar. It's not done. It's how we do things in England.' She raised a hand to her throat and tried to smile, wishing Fairley had travelled with her. She could have done with a bit of tea and sympathy.

'The signore comes?'

There she went. The inquisitive old maid was asking about Angus again. Why he stayed away so much, why he did not seem to come to her bed at night. 'The signore is missing Cromer.'

'*Come*?'

Geraldine explained. 'My husband misses his valet. We are looked after rather differently in England. But he has found a band of Englishmen he likes to spend time with, Mamma Clara. By the time they are done with cards and whisky and cigars, it's quite late and he is exhausted.'

'*Esausto.*'

'Exactly. And remember, this is Venice—he's got to get about on foot. It makes everything fatiguing.'

'There was a boy, signora.'

'A boy?'

It took some time, and a great deal of hand gestures, for Mamma Clara to make Geraldine understand a message had been sent by a boy. 'He run very much.'

'And what was the message?'

'Is downstairs.'

Geraldine was surprised the note or card was not brought up to her. And asking for it to be done would be too much. When she was dressed, she descended, to find Angus on his way to breakfast.

'Angus! Good morning. I thought you would look in.'

'Good morning, dear Geraldine. Let's breakfast together. There is a great deal to see in this amazing city. A thousand bridges, a million churches, wells in the middle of public squares, and people everywhere, on foot. One can hear languages spoken, aloud, from all over Europe. It is quite a place!'

'Where shall we go first?'

He handed her a brass tray full of cards and notes. 'There was a boy,' he said.

'So I was told—did he bring all this?'

'Apparently. Apparently news of our arrival preceded us, and many are eager to make our acquaintance.'

So the round of social interaction started. There

were a number of English residents in the city, and a number of temporary visitors on their Grand Tour, so it seemed that their time in the ancient city would be spent between afternoon calls, luncheons, dances, card parties and soirees.

'Tonight, a soiree. We need not go far. Sir Septimus and Mrs Alfington would like our presence, to listen to an Italian string quartet.'

'How lovely. Although it's not long since we left home, it would be a great pleasure to listen to a few words in English.'

Angus enjoyed the social whirl of the next fortnight much more than Geraldine did. Coming from the country, she was used to a quiet life, with occasional visits made and received from friends they knew well, two hunts a year, perhaps a season in London, and a lot of vigorous riding, which she sorely missed. She wanted to converse with her father, to learn more about the running of Denisthorn. She wanted to ride on the estate, looking at it with new proprietary eyes.

'When shall I ever see a horse again?'

Angus laughed, thinking she jested. 'Ah, you and your riding. You might put it all behind you, dear Geraldine.'

'I certainly hope not! It will be the first thing I do when we return to Denisthorn Hall.'

The music that evening was very good, but not all the people gathered there were aware of the fact. Conversation buzzed even during the concerto movements, which was unusual.

Geraldine decided to enjoy it anyway, and to put

on an absorbed expression to signal her avid fascination with the music and discourage any chat. During a brief break, she turned to acknowledge a young woman who had just taken an empty seat by her side.

'You must think me forward, Lady Crownrigg, but this is Venice, and things are done quite differently here. So I am allowed, by sheer necessity, to introduce myself.' She held out a hand. 'I am Sofia Bridwell. Do you mind if I sit near you for a while?'

'I am so very glad to make your acquaintance, Miss Bridwell. How are you finding the music?'

The young woman nodded and smiled. 'During any stay in Venice, one cannot escape the works of Vivaldi. I am so glad these musicians are particularly good.' She leaned closer. 'There is a very insistent gentleman. He has followed me around the room today, and quite robbed me of any peace and solitude at yesterday's garden party at Madame Deschamps.'

Geraldine looked around. 'Oh, stay by me. I think I see him. We can listen to the music together. People are not tending to keep to their seats.'

When the piece was finished, they rose together and walked to a balcony railing on which a climbing plant covered in blue flowers spilled to the ground.

'Oh, I wonder what this is. I have never seen anything like it.'

'A clematis, I think. Look closer. If we appear to be fully engrossed, your young man might not interrupt us.'

Sofia Bridwell laughed. 'He is certainly not my young man. I much prefer the company of women. I fail to see the attraction in men. They smell.'

Geraldine looked round at her, eyes wide.

'They do, Lady Geraldine! Cigars, strong drink, sweat. I should rather prefer to sit next to a stableboy than a gentleman. At least with the boy, the smell would have a just cause, an honest reason.'

'Do you ride, Miss Bridwell?'

The young woman nodded and smiled. 'Not in Venice, of course. We run a nice stable in England. My mother, rest her soul, was an excellent horsewoman, since a child. Grandfather ran thoroughbreds, so we are a very horsey family.'

'Thoroughbreds!' Geraldine was fascinated. 'Tell me more.'

'Well, from just one Arabian stallion, on loan for breeding purposes, my grandfather produced numbers of mounts, most for use as racehorses, but for the cavalries as well.' She put a hand up to shield her words. 'And two or three for royalty.'

They talked horses and riding until they could hear the music, which drew them back to the house. Taking their seats quietly, they enjoyed an Albinoni piece. Talk then fell to Baroque music, with which Geraldine was not familiar.

'We have so much to talk about, Miss Bridwell.'

'And we cannot do it all in Venice. I pray, do come and visit us at Cleeve Park.'

'Cleeve Park! Is that anywhere near Cleeve Hill?'

'Grandfather's stud is north of that. He is no longer with us. Mamma, when she was with us, and my father, Sir Bernard Bridwell, run the establishment.' She seemed quite proud of the goings-on at Cleeve Park. 'Father had a new house built. It took a long time, but it is very modern and light and bright. I quite like it. I wish that you could see it, and also the stables and yards. Do say you will visit.'

'Cleeve Hill is no great distance from us at Denisthorn Hall. What a happy coincidence, to be meeting you here in Italy.'

'This is my second visit, but I hope to go somewhere else next time. I think I should see something other than bridges and churches.' She sighed. 'And streets made of water. And going everywhere on foot or by gondola.'

'You seem to understand the customs. Why are the back doors of houses used? We come and go through the back door!'

'Well, Lady Crownrigg, back doors are street doors, used when one leaves and arrives on foot. Have you noticed a space leading off the entry, called the *androne*?'

'Yes, it seems to be a large hall, with no fireplace, and sometimes—as in this house—an excess of decoration. Enough sculpture for a museum.'

Miss Bridwell laughed. 'Venetians are known for impractical ornamentation. The big palace near where you are lodged, Palazzo Grimani, is destined to become a museum, they have been saying for years. It has a grand entrance, and an enormous, ornate *androne*.'

'So all houses have an *androne*?'

'All the grand residences which face onto a canal. If you have observed, the *androne* has a large, sometimes arched, front door. But it leads to the water entry, at which one leaves and arrives by boat. There is a covered dock, and huge doors, whose bottom is more often than not submerged.'

'I am so glad you have explained away that

mystery. I am also grateful that our lives in England are not so complicated.'

'They might seem so to Venetians. The servants where I am staying do not understand afternoon tea.' She gave a bold laugh and furled her fan. 'To them it might seem an incomprehensible complication!'

Delighted that they were less than a day's carriage drive from each other in England, the two women parted friends, promising to write to each other and visit.

Geraldine ended the day on a high note, full of optimism and delight at having made a friend with similar interests.

Angus was less than pleased that his wife spent a great deal of the time talking to just one person, but he made no fuss about it, and planned to pass the evening at cards again, after a supper at the Baglioni.

'The Baglioni? What is the Baglioni? Is it a club?'

'No, my dear. It is one of the oldest hotels in Venice. It has history, and not a small amount of luxury, I am told, so I am eager to try it out together with some chaps. And I shall return quite late, so please do not wait up for me. I shall return *on foot*, of course.'

'So you will not be coming to our lodgings? Am I to dine alone again?' Geraldine was surprised. But she took it in good grace after her agreeable conversation with Sofia Bridwell. She walked back to the Harling house at a leisurely pace, in the company of two other ladies who were staying in the same neighbourhood, and received the sweet attention of both Mamma Clara and her daughter Tonietta, who brought out another unusual but delectable repast.

Geraldine smiled as she committed the

unforgiveable by reading a newspaper at her solitary dinner table. She turned the pages as she ate a dish of lamb morsels, threaded onto fragrant rosemary skewers. They seemed to have been cooked over open flames and served on a bed of herbs, which she was told was an ancient Venetian delicacy.

Relishing her solitude, she brushed away the initial resentment—and mystification—at Angus's behaviour on their honeymoon, preferring to be with his friends rather than with her, and took stock. She had not yet been married a month, and it was turning out rather differently from what she had expected, but she was happy. She was looking forward to a future occupied with Denisthorn Hall and its administration.

'I should be happy. I should be able to do what I please, while Angus does what he pleases. It is not a bad situation at all.' She took another mouthful, and turned another page.

It was the London Gazette, and it was more than a week old, but it drew her closer in her mind to her beloved England.

CHAPTER TWELVE

In which Mr Phineas Gow makes a move
and
Lady Croukerne is surprised in her own garden

The letter from the dowager marchioness lay on the breakfast table. Athena had read it once, quickly, giving a small gasp and turning to her cup of tea. She was not alone at table. Maud Blockley sat across from her, and Miss Purl lower down to the left. They enjoyed different breakfasts.

Athena, wanting to retain her silhouette, ate only a poached egg and half a muffin. Miss Blockley helped herself to a heaped plate of kedgeree from the sideboard, and then two pieces of toast and marmalade, exclaiming as she did that the preserves in London were a mere pale imitation of the delicious jams, pickles and marmalades available at their country houses. Miss Purl ate quietly, delving with great enjoyment into some scrambled eggs, a tomato, and a buttered kipper.

'Has your post dismayed you in some way, Athena?' Miss Blockley looked up when she noted the silence, in which the sound of horse traffic from the street could be heard. 'Has something untoward happened?'

'Nothing like that, Maud. Nothing has happened. The only untoward thing this morning is my grandmother's letter.' She used her serviette, put it back on her lap, and took the last forkful of egg. The footman had left the teapot conveniently to her right, so she poured herself another cup and sat back slightly.

'Is there news?' Miss Purl was curious, but not curious enough to ask specific questions. Her own post conveyed the news that yet another of her aged uncles had passed away, but she had so many, her mother having been one of eleven children, and her father one of nine, that she had trouble trying to visualise the face or features of the newly deceased. In any case, the letter said there was no need to travel to her home county, since the funeral had already taken place, and the journey to the Scottish Borders much too long and gruelling.

'No news, just opinions, Miss Purl. And perhaps you know how irritating I find arbitrary opinion, even if it comes from someone as revered, venerable and elderly as my grandmother.'

Maud was not backward in inquiring. 'What has she opined about? Surely it is accession. Some people believe Prince Albert not to be a suitable heir to the throne. And seeing our dear queen's advanced age, and infirmity, accession is being debated up and down the country.'

'Prince Albert,' said Athena, lowering her voice lest anyone else would hear what she had to say, 'will accede, whether or not any of us think him a suitable king. My goodness, it has been a very long time since we had a king, and perhaps that might bring about a few good changes.' She raised her voice slightly. 'But it was not that. My grandmother is acting like a bridesmaid.'

'A bridesmaid!' The two other ladies exclaimed at

once.

Athena's cheeks reddened. 'Yes, I'm afraid so. She is—metaphorically speaking, of course—treading on my bridal train. She is hurrying me onward toward marriage. And my reaction, my response ...'

'Your response?' Both her companions spoke at once again, and turned to smile at each other for thinking the same thing.

'My response can only be—and it will be written in a letter to Grand-mama this afternoon—that I must wait for a proposal. I have to wait for a suitor to address my father, and ask for my hand. A whole season has nearly gone past, and I have not seen a single sign of anything of that nature. But there is little I can do.' She put a hand to her breast. 'Whereas you, Maud, have attracted quite a lot of attention, and a proposal ... which you have *accepted.*'

Miss Blockley simpered and put down her fork. 'Indeed I have. Walter and I ...'

'Oh dear. *Walter and I.* You sound as though you are already wedded, Maud. And you are merely betrothed.'

'I would never say *merely* about something so important,' her friend answered, not being in the least offended. She knew now why Athena said some pointed things. It was because she was envious. And being envied by one so pretty, so slender, and so well-connected gave her a great deal of satisfaction. 'I am engaged. Marriage is a unique undertaking.'

'Even though so many, almost everyone, marries.' Athena turned and stood, going to peer between folds of the sheer curtains. 'It is not so rare a thing, nor is it unique. Nearly everyone does it. The privilege is going to pass me by, I'm afraid.'

'Don't be too sure of that,' offered Miss Purl. 'You're still young enough to enjoy a whole other season, next year, and reap rewards.'

'Next year! I should surely be a confirmed spinster by then. It is simply years since I was presented at St James's. And Geraldine would have been married an *age*, and will no doubt become a matron, with a child in her lap! I run the danger of becoming an aunt before I am a wife.'

Athena was to remember the sentence she uttered at breakfast in the afternoon. The ladies were once more ensconced in the small sitting room after a late luncheon, all occupied with some sort of needlework. Miss Blockley had just finished playing two brief etudes by Czerny at the piano.

Athena was distracted, mentally scolding herself for being so disloyal to Maud Blockley by thinking that she and Walter Phisgrove were not an appropriate physical match, he being so tall and thin and Maud having the rounded English plump peach appearance that made them look lopsided. She bade herself be more affectionate and respectful of her friend. 'What a silly, silly fool I am becoming,' she said aloud.

Neither of the other ladies had time to ask Athena why she said that, because Hayes the footman announced Mr Phineas Gow.

'Again!' Maud Blockley fluttered her fan. 'Perhaps the gentleman has time to kill while in London, and this is the closest house to his club!'

He was greeted, and Athena rang for tea. For

fifteen minutes, talk centred around the Isle of Wight, and how often the queen seemed to travel there, and how she loved Osborne House.

'Lady Athena, may I beg your ear for just a few minutes?' Mr Gow was nothing if not perfectly correct.

'Of course, Mr Gow. Would you like to follow me to the library?' Athena led the way to the room where her father saw to his papers when he was in London. That day, he was away at the House of Lords. She was sure Mr Gow wanted to leave something for her father with her.

'Every time I visit, Lady Athena, I cannot help thinking how similar our views are. Your views on the royal family exactly dovetail mine. Every time I pass a shop window, I see something you might like. Every time I take a stroll in Hyde Park, I think how pleasant it would be to walk there together.'

'Together, Mr Gow!' Athena's heart skipped a beat. The ugliest man in England was waxing lyrical in her father's London library.

'You must have noticed, Lady Athena, that I cannot stay away. This is my third or fourth afternoon visit. And I have often overstayed the proper fifteen to twenty minutes!'

'I have never noticed any impropriety, Mr Gow. I was only yesterday saying to my companions how ...'

'Indeed. And I am here today to ask if I may ... if I might ... If you would be displeased if I asked to see you, to write to you, to visit you, a lot more often.'

'More often, Mr Gow!'

Phineas Gow took Athena's hand. 'I should like to be able to see you every day.'

'Every day! What are you saying, Mr Gow?'

The nervous gentleman took out a braid-edged handkerchief and wiped his brow. He gazed as far as the shelves of books on the far wall, allowing a long silence to fall in the room.

It was in that silence that Athena confirmed to herself what was about to happen. She held her breath. This was going to be a momentous day, one she would remember for a long time; a proposal from the ugliest man in England. She almost tittered to herself. Whatever would her mother, Lady Croukerne, think? Whatever would be the reaction of the dowager marchioness, her grandmother? Could she guess what the gossip might be like?

'I am saying, Lady Athena,' proceeded Mr Gow. 'I am saying … I am asking whether you would consider me as your husband. Whether you'd consent to be my wife. To consent to me talking to Lord Croukerne as soon as I possibly can.' The words took a great effort. The man was moved and close to being agitated. His excitement was palpable. He was as out of breath as if he had run up two flights of stairs.

Athena was struck dumb. Only that day at breakfast she had felt she would give up, that no one would ever ask her hand in marriage. She raised fingers to lips and blinked.

'I should understand, Lady Athena, if you require some time to consider the question, seeing that it comes completely out of the blue.'

'It does, Mr Gow. It does. It's a bolt of lightning out of a clear sky.'

'I am sure you never once considered the possibility that I might be rather taken with—ah, very taken with you. With the way you speak, your intelligence, and your interest in business and banking.'

'I must admit it crossed my mind, but ...'

The man's face fell.

'But? Ah. We must wait to see what Lord Croukerne says. Is that what you mean? Would you consent to me speaking to him, Lady Athena? But wait—you *must* need some time to think.'

Athena took a deep breath. She blinked, keeping her eyes shut for a brief instant. Her mind raced, her pulses beat a staccato rhythm. How was she to give a proper response? 'I do not need time to think, Mr Gow.'

The man's face fell again. He took a step back. 'Have I been too forward? Have I been presumptuous? Precipitate?'

Athena smiled. 'Oh, do not apologise. Please. No, you have been perfectly circumspect and proper, Mr Gow. There are no problems in that regard.'

'So ...'

'So I do not need time to think, Mr Gow. Phineas—my answer is yes.'

His face brightened. If the ugliest man in England could be said to take on a handsome light, then this was the moment. He released Athena's hand, and fumbled, took it in his again, and kissed it. 'Yes?'

Athena lowered her eyes. Her cheeks reddened.

'Yes?' He asked again.

'It's almost as if you cannot believe me, Phineas.'

'I almost cannot, Athena.'

'I think you must hurry away now, and return when Papa comes home. This evening, perhaps?'

The man stood back one step, and bowed formally.

'Of course.'

Athena leaned forward. She took his arm. 'You might have forgotten something, Phineas.'

For a moment, Mr Phineas Gow seemed perturbed. Then he saw what his young companion meant. Taking that step forward again, he leaned in and kissed her gently on the cheek.

She beamed. 'I think we have an understanding.'

'I think we do, Athena.'

It took a few minutes for her to recover. What had she done; what had she accepted? She must be crazy. But no; here was a man who—despite being her senior by more than a decade—was gentle, kind, and a proper gentleman. Not only that. He was affluent and well-fixed.

She opened the double doors to the sitting room, where her companions waited. Neither of them suspected that Mr Gow had anything to say to her apart from business with her father or with her brother-in-law Angus Crownrigg.

'We can return to the country!' she announced. 'Our sojourn in London is over.'

They both looked at her in calm surprise.

Lady Edwina Croukerne took a turn in the garden, with a flat flower basket, quite empty, looped through her arm. A pair of scissors hung loosely in her fingers. Her eyes gazed upward, to a perfect sky decorated with a few cottonwool clouds. 'I do declare it is perfect. My house is perfect, my life is perfect. Were it not for Ninian's condition, everything would be perfect. One daughter married, and another—perhaps with another season in London—not too far away from finding a suitable husband.'

Only that morning she had remarked to her lady's maid Prudhomme that she felt light of heart. Lady Croukerne did not know it, but the maid was relieved to hear it, and pleased that there was no mention of the little baron, whose death was now some time behind them. Her mistress was subject to swings of mood. She went from bright and optimistic to cramped with doubt, prey to visions of her dead little boy running around in a green jacket, or playing with his hoop, or asking for a bicycle.

'Oh, if only Ninian could take a turn around the garden with me.' Edwina Crownrigg brushed fingers against the petals of a rose. 'The roses are *perfect*.'

But Lord Croukerne was in the big library, in conference with Lewis Swinnart and another agent. Two big books, open to their latest entries, lay on his desk, and a stern expression twisted his face.

'My lord, I am sure ...'

Ninian Crownrigg held up a hand. 'No, no, no, Swinnart. Just a minute, if you please. Before you launch into a long description, or narration, or whatever it might be, I would like to make an observation. I might be confined to this wheelchair, but I still must make important decisions.'

'My lord, of course.'

'And it is trying, severely trying, to wrestle with the figures, trying to find mathematical solutions. I was used to tramping about, riding around, and looking at things for myself. Now I must rely on you men to report to me, and we do not always see things in the same light.'

'No, my lord. I mean yes, yes.'

'I realize we cannot always see eye to eye, but here is a list of things,' he shook a sheet of paper in one hand. 'This list is comprehensive, and I do understand the urgency of all the inclusions. But it stands to reason that we cannot, simply cannot, do it all at once. It's simply not feasible.'

'My lord, of course.' Both men knew that Mr Angus Crownrigg's wealth would be added to the fluidity of the Denisthorn account. But they did not bargain for the circumspection of their master.

'You say *of course*, and yet you hand me a long list that would take many thousands of pounds to execute.'

'My lord, we have ridden around for a week trying to form priorities.' The other agent, with cap in hand, tried to form something into one simple sentence that would not alarm his master.

'Lloyd, thank you. I should appreciate it if you both went away and drew up a much shorter list of absolute priorities. And appreciate if one of you would arrange with my man Thorn to wheel me to inspect some of the ones closer to home. In the next couple of days.'

'My lord.'

'Good then—we can leave it there for now.'

Swinnart looked at his boots, then stared at a wall of books, then looked Lord Croukerne in the eye. 'In the beginning, your lordship, I thought I could come up with ...'

Afraid that his agent would launch into another long speech, a veritable maze of words he would have to find his way through, Lord Croukerne raised his hand and stopped him. 'Now if one of you could summon

Thorn, I should spend some time attending to personal correspondence.'

His valet was at the door.

'Ah, Thorn. Be the man and wheel me out to the back terrace. I must clear my head before I start on my letters. It is crammed with figures for which I have no stomach this morning. Everything has become so frightfully expensive. Everything is so very difficult.'

'Everything is, your lordship.' It could not be said that Thorn ever disagreed with his master.

'And I find keeping the books and deciphering costs and calculating amounts to be the most difficult of all.'

They arrived at the terrace, and Thorn placed the wheelchair at an angle so the sun would not shine directly into Lord Croukerne's eyes.

'Why, that is Lady Croukerne, my lord. And she seems to be in something of a hurry.'

'Yes, Thorn, she is heading this way. Well, perhaps you'll give us a few minutes.'

Thorn backed his way through the French windows into the house and disappeared.

Ninian Crownrigg, Lord Croukerne, fifth earl of Denisthorn and Baron Brockworth knew that his wife was becoming a bit unpredictable in her moods. He did not want his valet to witness whatever disposition she was in today, because she looked rather agitated. She had been fine in the morning, seeming to be approaching a happy frame of mind. But when her face came into focus, he could see that her eyes were full of something approaching consternation.

'Ninian, Ninian!'

He sighed. He had hardly been back from London two days, and already he was faced with problems of a financial nature on the estate, with urgent repairs to the stables and the leaks in the roof being foremost among many, and now the ever changeable quality of his wife's temperament.

'My dear. You seem to have encountered some frightening creature. A vole, perhaps ... or at least a spider.'

'Do not patronise me, Ninian. I will not have it. Something untoward is happening, and as master of this house I think you should know.'

'Not *another* problem.' He sighed. 'And I thought you were hurrying my way to say the roses have had their second flush.'

'Stop it, I say—stop it, Ninian!'

'What's happening then?'

'Athena is back from London.'

'We came back together, my dear, and have been here two days.'

Out of breath, Lady Croukerne climbed the last two steps and looked down at her husband. She looked back towards the French windows and to either side, to make sure no one was listening. 'Ninian, Athena is in the rose bower with Mr Phineas Gow!' She took two quick breaths and placed a hand at her waist. 'This is most inappropriate. Ninian—please listen!'

'I am listening. I do know Mr Gow is here. Mrs Beste knows he will be joining us for luncheon.'

'She does?'

'I know, my dearest. I do.'

'You do! You do? Our daughter is in the rose bower

with Mr Gow, and I saw them ... I saw them *kissing*!'

'Calm down, Edwina.'

'I shall not calm down. Your daughter, Ninian! Your daughter and the ugliest man in England. He's old enough ...' She took a deep breath, and the words exploded from her. 'He is old enough to be her father!'

'Not quite, but I see what you say. He is not a great deal younger than I am, that is true. But his intentions are sincere.'

'How could you possibly know his intentions!'

'Because we spoke for a quarter of an hour, just before the agents came into the library. He arrived by coach early, after breakfast, driven from the station.' He looked at his wife's face. 'And I must say I was happy to receive him.'

'You spoke!'

'We did indeed. He has asked Athena to marry him, and she has accepted.'

'*Ninian!*'

'Edwina. It's fine. Athena seems to be quite happy, and I have given them my blessing. Mr Gow—Phineas— is an honourable man. And,' he turned away to look far across the garden to the mirror lake. 'And I think they'll make a fine couple.'

'Ninian—what have you done?'

'Do you listen to anything your daughter says, Edwina?'

'What do you mean?'

'Exactly what I said.'

'She speaks in stutters. In sentences of two words!'

'Not any longer.' Lord Croukerne reminded his wife that for some time, Athena had said she wanted to marry someone wealthy, someone prosperous, with the ability to invest well and create more wealth. She wanted a notable establishment, a beautiful house with plenty of servants, and never have to worry again about pounds, shillings and pence. And there she was, having netted herself one of the most prosperous men they had ever known.

'But he has no title!'

'He has money, Edwina. He is a barrister.'

'But he's Angus's *uncle*.'

'He has money. And young Angus will inherit my title, and ...' he spread both hands wide. '... all this at Denisthorn Hall, and its accompanying problems. He has money too, so it will all resolve itself.'

'Ninian!'

'Both our girls have done well, my dear. Both Geraldine and Athena have done well.'

'But how could Athena ... he has the most alarming features. His nose ...'

'Edwina!'

She held a hand up to her lips and looked towards the rose garden. 'Here they come, arm in arm. Look! Arm in arm. My older daughter and the ...'

'And the most suitable husband. Now be sure to be happy for them, my dear.'

'But to be surprised in my own garden!'

'And what a happy surprise, eh?' Lord Croukerne shifted in his wheelchair, in pain for the first time that day, and waved to his smiling daughter and her fiancé.

Chapter Thirteen

*In which another wedding is planned at Denisthorn Hall
and
Lady Geraldine confirms a suspicion*

Lady Margery and Sir Herbert stood still and stiff. On paying a visit to Denisthorn Hall, they were given the full news of Athena's engagement.

'I told Ninian a hundred times, but he will not listen to me,' Lady Croukerne said to her sister when they moved from the hall to the day sitting room. 'He says Athena is a clever headstrong woman who likes to get her way. She's not the young girl we remember, who grumbled and mumbled one-word retorts. She has acquired the ability to speak up for herself, Ninian says. And she certainly knows what she wants. She has not demurred once.'

'I perceived some changes as she matured. When she stayed with us, she seemed tongue-tied, but I saw progress.'

'How can we call this progress? I fear for her happiness.'

'Perhaps,' Sir Herbert said, slowly and deliberately, 'that is what she will find with Mr Gow.'

His wife did not seem to agree. 'But Angus's *uncle*, Edwina! How can she marry so mature a man? How could she be happy with such an age difference? What will people say?'

Lady Croukerne fluttered her hands in the air and let them fall in her lap. 'Ninian says it doesn't matter at all what people say, as long as Athena is content. At the moment, she is blissful.'

'Blissful?'

'She's walking on air. She is full of smiles. I don't know what has got into the girl. I have never seen her so bright and cheerful.'

Sir Herbert looked at his wife and her sister. 'Margery, I suppose all girls are happy when they have just got engaged.'

'All of them? I don't remember Geraldine being *blissful*. I recall her indecision, her doubt. I remember her in tears on more than one occasion.'

'Geraldine is a personality unto herself, isn't she?' Lady Croukerne's eyes grew wide. 'I have written to her, post haste. Because they must return from Italy sooner than planned, mustn't they?'

Lady Margery's eyes were wider than her sister's. 'Why? Why such undue haste? Have they named a day, Athena and this Mr ... Mr ...?'

'Mr Phineas Gow.'

'Tongues will wag if there's a hurried plan.' Lady Margery's brow creased. 'Surely there will be a wait of at least six months. Have you spoken to old Lady Croukerne? There are so many things to arrange and order and ...'

'I know, Margery. Haven't we just had Geraldine's wedding? Now that took a lot of preparation. I never cease to thank heaven I have staff that can cope with important events. Mrs Jones, our cook, is a miracle on legs, I do declare!' She clapped her hands in delight. 'Grand-mama Croukerne is delighted to hear of Athena and Mr Gow, because she's a great believer in expediency. And little Frederic will so enjoy a second taste of a big wedding cake.'

'Edwina!'

Sir Herbert made a grave expression, but shook his head at his wife to silence her. He half raised a finger to his lips, feeling, no doubt, that it would not do to upset Margery's sister and shake her out of her good mood. 'I might look for Ninian, then, and let you ladies chat about gowns and wedding feasts.' He rose and left the room.

Sir Herbert's brother-in-law was in the library. He shut a large ledger with a slap when he saw there was company. 'Herbert! Have you been told all the details of our good news?'

'We were surprised to get your note with the announcement. You haven't put it in the paper yet, have you?'

'It will appear on Saturday.'

'So soon. Have you thought about this properly, Ninian?'

They discussed the engagement seriously, their heads together. Sir Herbert was asked to pour two brandies, which he did, after which he seemed a bit more receptive to Lord Croukerne's rationale.

'Mr Phineas Gow has enough resources to buy Athena whichever property she sets her eyes on. She wants something grand in the country. I believe he has a nice town house in Edinburgh, and Athena has only to ask for a London house. The manner and style in which she will live is assured.'

'Goodness! How much is the man worth? How could a barrister have such liquidity?'

'Apparently he is much in demand. His chambers are very busy. He employs a number of clerks. Besides, he is an excellent investor, and is involved in banking as well. He did explain Angus's enviable position to me when he and Geraldine were engaged, and in doing so, also revealed a certain amount of information about himself. He's a gentleman, Herbert.'

'You do need the full picture, Ninian. You must avoid exposing your older daughter to ruin!'

Lord Croukerne laughed. 'Far from ruin. As far from ruin as it is possible to be. Mr Gow called on me after Athena accepted him. He was prompt in doing so. Alacrity and honesty are that gentleman's strong points. And he divulged his entire worth to me in five or six minutes.'

'Well—we met him at Geraldine's wedding. I cannot say I was overly impressed.'

Ninian Crownrigg leaned forward. 'Now, now, Herbert. Do not stoop to mention the man's visage! Edwina could speak of nothing else when she heard the news. She calls him the ugliest man in England!' Lord Croukerne gave a mirthful grunt. 'But he is of fine figure. He is hale and hearty and full of energy.'

Sir Herbert made to open his mouth.

'And do not do me the disservice of agreeing with Edwina, I beg you, Herbert. It has nothing to do with anything. If Athena sees fit to let his appearance go by the by, I do not think we have the right to make observations of that superficial nature to her.'

'I must say, Ninian, that I admire your integrity. And also your attention to your daughters' wishes.' He finished his brandy. 'But not only is the man not the handsomest on earth, but one can hardly understand him when he speaks.'

'He is Scottish, Herbert. And Athena understands him perfectly. Ah—here she is!'

Athena swept into the library. She looked in fine spirits, her cheeks heightened, her eyes bright. 'Uncle Herbert, what a pleasure to see you! I take it Mama has Aunt Margery ensconced in the sitting room.'

Sir Herbert rose. 'Hearty congratulations, my dear! Hearty congratulations to you both. It pleases me to see you so happy.'

She laughed. 'I am, I am! And all after thinking for the whole London season that I would age a spinster. I never thought I should be planning my wedding so soon.' She looked at her father. 'You will have to roll up the aisle again, Papa, with Thorn right behind you, and Cosmo on a leash, waiting outside with a groom!'

'Indeed. And the house will once more be in sixes and sevens in preparation.' He rued all the confusion and upheaval, but he said the words with a smile. It was so unusual to see his older daughter in high spirits that he felt he would do anything to extend her joy.

'Is Mr Gow still in London, or has he travelled back to Edinburgh?'

'He is in Chester, of all cities, to see a famous jeweller, because he is ordering a ring. For me—an engagement ring! And he's drawing up papers, together with a lawyer, to assist Angus. You do know they are opening a bank branch in Cheltenham. It is all rather complicated, and I don't know the *first* thing about their business, but it bodes well.'

'It does bode well, my dear. Perhaps in the future you will be spending your time between the three cities yourself.'

Athena settled in an armchair. 'Not in Cheltenham. I have my eye on a beautiful house which has just come vacant, outside Tredington. Phineas is rather keen for us to view it soon. If it all goes well, and if I like it ... do you know it? It's called Temple Grove.'

'Temple Grove! Yes, of course. But it's on a rather small parcel of land. And Tredington is not exactly a bustling place.'

She smiled. 'We would intend it to be a nice pied-à-terre, rather than a country seat. It's close to the village, on a rise overlooking a wood and a stream. Phineas has written me a long letter full of ideas, some of which are very agreeable.'

'How exciting, my dear.'

'Then there is his established home in Edinburgh, which I am eager to see. There will be changes made there.'

Sir Herbert remembered Phineas Gow was a widower, so his niece would want to redecorate to her own taste, and remove any traces of a former wife's selections. 'What about London?'

Athena looked at her father.

'I should be more than delighted for you both to stay in the Belgrave house whenever you are in London, my dear.'

'Thank you, Papa.' She sighed. 'There is so much to think about that I do declare my head is spinning.'

'It could not spin for a better or more delightful reason, dear Athena.' Lord Croukerne seemed just as joyful as his daughter.

Below stairs, there were dropped jaws and surprised exclamations. The servants' hall buzzed with talk. The piano playing paused. The female servants out-talked the men.

'Another wedding, so soon!'

'Doesn't one expect so? With Lady Geraldine being younger, and married off first, it's no surprise that Lady Athena would hurry up and make a match.'

Maisie the housemaid shook her head. 'I do wish they'll wait a while before announcing the day. We were well and truly run off our feet last time.'

'Come on, Maisie—all that extra help came in from the village.' One of the footmen laughed at her.

She bridled and laughed back. 'Have you already forgotten the number of rugs you rolled, Peter Formby? Have you completely forgotten the heavy trays, the number of times you changed your gloves, the fetchin' and carryin', the number of times you wobbled on a ladder?' Her eyes were crinkled with humour.

'Maisie, you know you love it when the house is busy.'

'I do like a bit of activity, I do. We go too long in this house with nothin' happenin' at all. Even last November's hunt was cancelled.'

'His lordship was not up to a hunt!'

'Does Lady Athena's new fiancé hunt?'

'I don't imagine he does. I cannot imagine him on

horseback.'

'He seems energetic and healthy. He is not unduly portly, either.'

'But I cannot see that face riding a horse.' Maisie laughed out loud.

'How do you know what he looks like?'

'Oh, I watched from behind the baize door the first time he arrived.'

'Now Mr Crownrigg—he's a good horseback rider. But this new gentleman—he's not far in age from his lordship. And have you seen him? He is rather full-bodied and ...'

'How could a skivvy ever hope to see *anyone*? People come and go, and I must scurry around with pan and brush, with coal bucket and scoop, with rag and bucket, rushed off my feet, to get everythin' done before they catch a glimpse of me! I'm invisible. I'm as scarce as a used brandy glass seen upstairs in the morning—we're tidied away without delay!' Hattie pulled a face.

They all laughed.

'Woe be me if any gentleman or lady even catches sight of my skirt disappearin' around a doorway.'

Another footman struck a match and inhaled on a small pipe. 'I've heard,' he said quietly, between puffs, 'that he cannot by the longest stretch of the imagination be called handsome.'

'Bob Godwin, you're the king of understatement!'

'Is it true?' Susan's curiosity was roused.

'Not only is he hard to understand ...'

'Why?'

'He's Scottish, Maisie.'

She formed a large O with her mouth.

'And I've heard her ladyship call him ugly, in so many words.'

The housemaid's eyes were like saucers. 'Why would Lady Athena want an ...'

'Money, love.' Formby waggled his chin. 'Money. Mister Scotland is the richest man to ever set foot in this house.'

'*Form-by?*' The resounding voice of Mr Herring, the butler, broke in on the convivial conversation.

Maisie was about to ask about money, but the butler's entry into the hall made her scurry away as if he were one of the gentlemen upstairs. The first words of the butler's scolding grew further away. She quickly rounded the corner near the bottom of the service stairs, dived past the housekeeper's office and took a breath only when she reached the boot room.

Once in there, she could tidy away a few rags, put the lids back on some tins of polish, place brushes back on their racks, and walk at a sedate pace to the drying room for a clean apron. 'Those boys better learn to do their own tidyin'. That boot room was a proper muddle.' She tied a bow behind her back. 'How hard could it be to put a few things away after polishing a pair of boots, I ask you.'

There was no one to ask.

Looking at her hands, she saw her nails needed a scrub, and remembered one of the other maids describing Lady Geraldine's engagement ring. An amber stone surrounded by diamonds, she said. Diamonds! She would never come within yards of diamonds. What would Lady Athena's ring be like then, if her intended was such a rich man?

Miss Sofia Bridwell looked well and shapely in a new silk evening dress adorned with a special kind of lace. An unusual shade of turquoise, the skirt swung well above the floor at the front, showing beautifully embroidered dancing slippers. 'This is Burano lace, Lady Crownrigg,' she held a hand up to shield her lips, and to suggest what she said next was private. 'I am told it's beautiful and the height of fashion while on tour.' Her face did not reflect what her words said.

They stood together at a ball, where many of the guests were of Italian and French nobility. Venetian musicians struck up, so they retreated to where they could hear each other's voices clearly.

'You do not favour it, I feel, Miss Bridwell. Perhaps you wear it to make your chaperone happy. Was the lace a gift?'

'That is so intuitive of you. She and her husband took me to the island of Burano to see it being finished. About a dozen women worked on it—quite an operation! How could I refuse?'

'It would have been ungracious. We all do and accept things to please relatives! This gown too was handstitched in our neighbourhood. I am not too fond of deep gathered lace edging on dresses, I'm afraid.'

'Remembering your other gown, I see you tend to like plain design. Fewer furbelows, I suppose. I would feel more comfortable in a riding habit, to be quite honest.'

'My thoughts exactly, Miss Bridwell. I should go so far as to suggest men seem a lot more comfortable. No stays, no tight shoes, no voluminous skirts. Have you ever thought …?'

The other woman tittered. 'Of course I have. I envy men their freedom. Freedom to move. Freedom from trappings made of *lace*. Oh, how I wish to be on horseback, free from furbelows.'

'I have not seen a horse for many weeks.' Geraldine looked sad. 'I sorely miss riding.'

'We should both be happier when we return home. Have you had any letters?'

'Two this morning, Miss Bridwell. There is good news from home, from Denisthorn Hall, which I miss so deeply. My sister Athena has accepted a proposal and is to be engaged. They might consider a wedding later this year. This means I must persuade my husband to return to England earlier than we planned.'

'You could not possibly miss your sister's wedding!'

'She is older than I am, so all our lives we thought she would be the first to marry. And look what has happened. Things develop differently to how everyone thinks they ought to, don't they?'

Miss Bridwell made a tacit question with her eyes.

'My husband Angus is to inherit my father's title.'

'Oh—that's unusual.'

'Not as rare as I thought. They are distant cousins. It happens when titles are not heritable except to males. It will change one day.'

'I'm certainly hopeful the whole world of laws will change to at least *include* women, consider us, remember we exist.' Did Miss Bridwell stamp her foot as she said that? 'Now tell me more about yourself.'

'Angus and I are third or fourth cousins. Papa has

explained it all to me, but it's complicated. I didn't know Cousin Angus existed until my father traced that side of the family.'

'How extraordinary!'

'And it all happened because our little brother Frederic succumbed to diphtheria.' Geraldine looked upward, then sidewards, trying to avoid her eyes filling with tears. It all happened suddenly, and it was many months ago, but it still stung. 'I so love Denisthorn Hall. I so adore my home and the estate, the countryside, the people that live around us and work for us. I would have done anything to keep it going, to keep it from falling to ruin. I want to be part of it until I die. I shall *not* be parted from my beloved home.'

Miss Bridwell took Geraldine's hand. 'Oh, you speak so strongly, even though you still suffer grief. You must need much consolation and succour from your husband. You have not been married long, which means you must have many things to relate to each other.'

'Consolation? Oh, I see what you mean. Well, Angus is a busy man.' Geraldine did not give an outright confession, not wanting to divulge personal business to a comparative stranger. Miss Bridwell seemed a good soul, one who would sympathise, but they were after all not close friends. It was something Geraldine wanted to change, especially after she learned they lived within reasonable distance in England, and shared a love of riding. But she knew friendship did not develop overnight.

As for consolation and succour from Angus, Geraldine knew he was not going to turn out to be the same kind of man as Lord Croukerne, who was sympathetic, and often offered his daughters a listening ear; who often took their part when there was a dispute with their mother. He could be stern and short-tempered when worried or in pain, but he was on the whole a patient man. Geraldine bit her lip. Perhaps kindness developed with age. She did not know much about that. It was true what Aunt Margery had said. The first year of a marriage was all about getting used to each other. So far, she learned that she had to get used to being left alone for a great deal of the time.

'Angus seems to prefer to spend time with his friends, playing cards. He also does a lot of business, even while we are here, on tour. He has spoken to a thousand bankers, and a thousand more businessmen, as he calls them. I suppose it is why his affairs run so smoothly and why he can afford this lifestyle. It is in fact not for me to say.'

'Do I sense a line of ...?' Miss Bridwell stopped.

Geraldine knew she was going to say *disappointment*, stopping just in time. 'Are they playing a waltz? Are you fond of a waltz?' They walked into the ballroom, which was a lavishly decorated space with ornate columns all around. The musicians played from a dais festooned with wide satin ribbons.

Moving to one side, because dancing had begun, Geraldine saw that Angus was already in the middle of the room, dancing with a young woman. They were surrounded by a host of other guests, but it was easy to see they were the first to emerge onto the dancefloor.

'Is that your husband, dancing with the daughter of the French ambassador?'

'Yes, Miss Bridwell. It is, it is. Although I did not

know who she is. Are you sure she is the daughter of an ambassador?'

'Definitely. They arrived in Venice on the same day as you. Now look at the lace on that gown.'

'We have not been introduced, but I see Angus is well ahead of me with his introductions.' She smiled and turned it into a jocular observation, and saw that her companion tittered and took it as such.

It was not a new discovery, but it confirmed Geraldine's realization that she was not of primary significance in her husband's mind. He did things without thinking. Or if he did think, it was to put his wishes and desires first. For Angus, it definitely appeared as though he would rather dance with the French ambassador's daughter than with his new wife.

She looked down at the rings on her left hand.

Miss Bridwell looked too. 'Without seeming too vulgar or curious, Lady Geraldine, I do admire your rings.'

'This is the engagement ring Angus ordered from Scotland. The centre stone is a cairngorm. I find it embarrassingly large.'

'It's quite beautiful. It will look well on your hand as the years go by. My mother always says that a large ring looks well on a mature hand.' She looked up. 'But here comes Mr Crownrigg.'

Angus approached and nodded acknowledgement to Miss Bridwell when they were introduced. 'Geraldine,' he said, as he took his wife's hand. 'This waltz?'

Because they did it so infrequently, Geraldine felt stiff and uncomfortable at first. She gradually relented to the rhythm. 'How are you enjoying the music, Angus?'

'I'm enjoying our sojourn here, but it's nothing like the atmosphere we have in England, is it? A lot of it seems too heightened. A bit false. Everything is overly ornamented. They serve food in strange removes.'

'I tend to agree. I laugh when I think I yearn for a plain boiled potato or slice of roast beef.'

'Oh. I thought you were enthusiastic and unwilling for it to come to an end.'

Geraldine sighed. She would have given anything to return home to the stables at Denisthorn Hall. 'I have received word. Athena and Mr Phineas Gow will soon name a day for their wedding. It would be extraordinarily fine if we could attend my sister's wedding. I should not like to miss it. What do you say, Angus?'

It was a while before he responded. Angus seemed to be humming with the music under his breath. Geraldine wondered if she would ever grow used to his ways. Would he insist they stay on and miss Athena's big day?

'Angus?'

'Geraldine. I do not often understand you.'

She held her breath. Was she to feel slighted at his words? Deciding to pause for more, for a fuller response, was the best expedient. There was a brief pause between melodies. He did not move away. She smiled and waited.

'I have ah ... great respect for your views, but I am often ah ... dumbfounded. *But this time*,' her husband continued, taking her in his arms once more for the next waltz, 'I do. I do understand. It is admirable that you would like to return to England for such an important event. Cousin Athena will be overjoyed.'

'You think so?'

'Yes, my dear.'

'You really do, Angus.'

'I've ah ... I've said so, haven't I? We shall abbreviate our stay in Venice, which will be easy to arrange, and return by steamboat to Marseilles. There, we shall rest a day. Then, we shall hasten to the ferry at Calais, by coach or by some means. I shall organize it. It's not a short journey, and might be uncomfortable, but we'll be on our way. Seeing England on the horizon from Calais should gladden both our hearts.'

A tide of happiness washed into Geraldine's heart. *Home!* 'Home, Cousin Angus. I cannot wait to arrive at Denisthorn.'

'Neither can I, Geraldine. Neither can I.'

So, her suspicions were confirmed. Angus longed to return to England just as much as she did. In that regard, they seemed well matched.

CHAPTER FOURTEEN

Mr Gow displays a generous character
and
Mrs Beste is deeply disappointed.
A new footman comes to Denisthorn

He arrived late in the afternoon, this time with his man. Mr Gow's arrival caused a stir, but on this occasion it was because he would be in the same house as his fiancée, which would not be tolerated, in polite society, for very long. Two days would be the most.

Below stairs, they called the visiting valet by his master's name, so the portly young fellow, who seemed to have grown a double chin even in his twenties, was welcomed. The butler, the footmen, and Thorn, his lordship's valet, gathered round.

'Welcome to Denisthorn Hall, Brown. We understand you are quite new in this positon with Mr Gow, due to an accident which took away your predecessor. Is that right?'

The man nodded, his face grave.

'In this house, below stairs, Brown, you will be called Mr Gow, after your master. You're only here for two days, so it will not be asking too much for you to share a room with our senior footman.'

'With Godwin, Mr Herring?' Formby was most surprised, seeing he had shared a room with Glover for such a long time.

'Yes. With Godwin. Thorn now sleeps close to his lordship's room near the library, in case he is needed in the night.'

'But I ...'

The butler raised an eyebrow. 'Wait until I complete what I have to say, Formby. From today onward Glover, as under-butler, can have his room to himself. So can Godwin, for the present, until more changes take place. Mr Crownrigg has his man, Cromer, who must also be accommodated. Formby—move yourself and your things immediately. You will be sharing with a new man, when he arrives.'

'So ...'

'So, let me finish.' The butler looked pointedly at the footman, then continued in his sonorous voice. 'Except when we have guests, such as tonight and tomorrow, Glover will occupy the first room along the men's passage, on his own.'

'You said there will be a new footman, Mr Herring.'

'Indeed. He will share with Godwin when he arrives. His name is Walker. And one of the girls who occasionally joins us from the village, Ivy Paine—we all know and like Ivy, she has worked at Cheltenham house on a number of occasions as well—will be sharing with Maisie up in the women's passage. That will be all. Please resume your tasks when you have given Mr Gow a cup of tea.'

The visiting valet was offered something with his tea, Maisie made sure of that. A plate of buttered teacake was quickly polished off, and the hall was soon deserted once more, with everyone away to a list of tasks.

'He is not a lean fellow, that Brown ... um, Mr Gow, as we are required to call him. One does notice his wide girth immediately, but he does seem light on his feet.' Maisie was particularly observant. 'He's new. Didn't Mr Gow visit without a servant before? I think I heard his valet left his employ without giving a reason.'

'He didn't say as much as a complete sentence, so we cannot know what happened, or what he's like.'

'Oh, he has a pleasant look in his eye.'

'Does it matter what kind of temperament he has, for two days?'

Maisie widened her eyes. 'Alice! *Think!* And do fold that properly, will you?' She went on. 'Mr Fin ... Phinn ... *whatever,* Gow is marrying Lady Athena. They will be back and forth between this house and theirs like shuttles at a Manchester cotton mill. We'd better learn to mind his ways.'

'The house is growing. There will be seven of us up there now.'

'It makes for a jolly house, although Susan and that girl Lizzie tend to be grumpy.'

'Wouldn't you be grumpy if you were wringing and hanging out wet linen all day? If you were ironin' all afternoon? If you were fillin' and emptyin' coppers and rinsin' troughs all the time? Those girls must have backs like whips not to be broken.'

'And arms like those of a boxer ... Susan does, anyway.' Maisie laughed.

'All this fuss and bother with engagements and weddings!'

'Only two daughters, love. Things will soon settle down, Alice. Now I envy Holly. That's who I'm jealous of.'

'Why? Just because she's a proper housemaid in a black dress and white apron, bonnet and cuffs? Because she's allowed around the house? She's run off her pins sometimes, when there are messages and flowers and calls for tea, tea, tea!' Alice clearly preferred her position of skivvy. She was forever washing things, sweeping, beating rugs out in the courtyard.

'Apart from Fairley, who is her lady's maid, Holly Walsh will be the one of few of us to see Lady Athena's engagement ring. I can't wait to hear her describe it.'

'The boys will see it.'

Maisie laughed. 'Have you ever heard an accurate description of anythin' about a lady's dress or hair or jewellery from one of the footmen? Huh! *Never*!'

Alice kept on folding table linen. 'Why do you think new people are being taken on?'

'On account of Lady Geraldine and Mr Angus, Alice, it's obvious. They'll be livin' here. Here, not in Scotland, as we thought. That's just one person more, and a valet, but look at it this way—we have two new big suites to look after. Being a young couple, they will have visitors comin' and goin'.'

'I suppose so.'

'Word is that Mr Angus is a sociable person, and likes his gatherings. Card parties, and so on. They'll probably have soirees and dinners and ... ooh,' she raised the back of a hand to her forehead. 'The November hunt will be on again. Makes me dizzy just thinkin', Alice.'

'Doesn't take much to make you dizzy.' Alice dug

her elbow into her companion's ribs and laughed.

'I'm just thinkin' of Christmas! It will be something else, wait and see.'

Dinner on the night Mr Gow arrived was delayed for ten minutes. It did not seem to matter to Lord Croukerne, nor yet for his wife, who came down the beautiful main staircase in a grey and lilac evening dress. But Lady Athena was nowhere to be found. Her mother opened the door to each sitting room and to the library.

Lord Croukerne emerged into the hall, where the central chandelier was blazing and a token fire glimmered in both fireplaces. Thorn pushed the wheelchair with some alacrity, thinking they were late. They had not heard the gong.

'Did you hear the gong, my dear?'

'Oh, Ninian. There you are. No, I did not, because it was not sounded. Athena asked me, so I requested Herring to delay for ten minutes. It should sound ... ah, there he comes now.'

Lord Croukerne suddenly realized what was going on. He held up a hand. 'Wait, Herring. Wait. Allow us to get to the small sitting room, and give us enough time for one sherry. Please.'

'One sherry, your lordship. Very well. I shall come in and serve you myself.' His face was neutral, passive, but anyone who knew Herring would guess he was not happy about the breaking of his routine.

'Ninian, why are you delaying further? The kitchen will be in an uproar. We have a guest.' Lady Croukerne was puzzled.

'That's just it, my dear. 'Let's allow our guest a moment to do what he has come here to do.'

The kitchen was not in an uproar, but the potatoes were sent down from the servery to the warming oven, and Cook knew the sauce over the fish would form a skin if delayed much longer.

'The minute you hear that gong, Formby. The *instant* you hear it, you run up those stairs. And don't forget the parsley. And the lemon! The *lemon* ...' She handed him a small dish of lemon wedges. Mrs Jones felt a bit deflated. She had been pleased the poached fish turned out the way it did; close to perfect, as perfect as it ever would be. And then there was a delay. 'It's not my lucky day,' she said to everyone in the kitchen, and no one in particular.

Her small neat figure was a slight bit bent; Cook was getting tired.

A sherry with Mrs Beste in her office would be welcome that evening. They usually had one when the kitchen maids were busy tidying and cleaning after the cooking was finished. They then waited for the dishes from the first course to come down so the girls could get started on the plates and cups and bowls. A footman attended to the glasses and Mr Herring did the knives, of course.

The boiler was full and humming, and Alice and another girl were already swishing the soap net through the first sink of water. Godwin came down from the servery with a laden tray of used dishes. 'Something's going on tonight. Is tonight special, then? Does anybody know?'

'Lady Athena's fiancé is here.'

'Well, I know *that*.'

'What could be more special?' Maisie wiped the cooking knives and lined them up, clean and sharp, on the wiped table, ready for the morning. 'Did you get a good look at the ring?'

'What ring?' Godwin looked at each face in turn. 'What ring?'

'See, Alice—I told you. Young men do *not* have a clue.'

In Mrs Beste's office, the smell of sherry was in the air. The two women sat side by side, tiny stemmed glasses in their hands.

'I've never been more disappointed in my life.'

'I thought you were a bit out of sorts, Mrs Beste. What happened? Has ... have you been let down then?'

'No, nothing like that. Nothing. I'm disappointed with myself. I don't know what came over me.'

'What happened?' Mrs Jones was sympathetic, and not a little curious. 'Is he no longer keen, then? What do you mean, disappointed with yourself?'

'Mr Pillow is as keen as ever, Cook.' She sighed. 'No one takes you to the tearooms and orders Eccles cakes and tea for two, standing there in a good sack jacket, too, if they are not *keen*.'

'So in what way ...?'

'I felt things were hurtling on too fast.'

'Too fast? Two years?'

'I had a sudden vision of occupying an estate cottage for retired servants, in Mr Pillow's company.'

'But that wouldn't happen for a while yet!'

'I'm not at retirement age, nor do I feel my energy flagging. But time flies, and I thought what marriage might mean at this late stage in my life. Why, I'm in middle-age. I'll be forty-three at the end of the year.'

Mrs Jones blinked. She did not know that Mrs Beste was younger than she was, and thought she had better conceal her years, in order not to be thought old by the staff, but more importantly by her employers. What would happen if her ladyship thought her too old to continue? She would have to hunt around for a few exceptionally good recipes.

'And the thought of living in a cottage with Mr Pillow was not attractive?'

'Oh, I don't know. What can I compare it to?' Mrs Beste's expression was wan and bland. 'I started as a kitchen maid, and worked under a very good cook. Like you, Mrs Jones.' Her face improved. 'I learned so much I became her assistant, and then under-housekeeper. They had them in those days. When this position came up, so many years ago now, I couldn't miss the opportunity. In those days, the old earl was still alive. You do remember. The dowager marchioness was exacting, so I learned how to be accurate.'

'And consistent. I remember her praising your *consistence*.'

They laughed together, remembering the past, when things seemed harder than now.

'All these things I might well be,' the housekeeper said with a wry grimace. 'But I have never been a wife. Everyone seems to think one's aim as a woman is to find a husband. I understand society's call. But I do not feel the call *myself*. I've been obeying a collective behest, without thinking.'

'*Collective behest*, eh? Where did you read that? Perhaps it's what all women do. Our young ladies upstairs seem to heed all that society demands of them. I've heard either one or the other say quite clearly, *It's not for me to say. It's not for me to decide.*'

'What shall I do?' Mrs Beste seemed quite confused.

'The last thing you should do is lead the man on. There's nobody more outraged than a man disappointed, if he thinks a sure thing comes to nothing.'

'So I should either continue and marry him, or stop now, is that your advice?'

Mrs Jones raised both hands and slapped them down gently on her lap. 'I listen to you, Mrs Beste, my dear. I lend a sympathetic ear, but I don't presume to offer you advice, never having been married myself.'

'So in that case, I need to make up my mind. And soon. And either enter a world of unknown quantities, or remain a spinster forever.'

Mrs Jones waggled her head. 'There's a positive side to that.'

'I can't see it!'

'I can see us, growing old, in a cottage on the estate, by grace and favour of the new earl.'

'What—you and I?"

'Yes.' Mrs Jones looked serious. 'Yes, you and I. We're not only engaged in the same house doing the important work. We don't only just get on. We've become firm friends, Kitty.'

'We have, we have. So there you are. You're both perceptive and clever, Anne. I can picture your setting much better than I can see me sharing my life with Mr Pillow!'

'Do you know, I see nothing wrong with that, and we should manage quite well in each other's company. But it's many years away, many years.'

'Just think of how many years Lady Geraldine has before her here, as future mistress of Denisthorn.'

'And Lady Athena not too far away. How young they are!'

They fell to talking about what had reached their ears about what happened in the library earlier that evening.

Athena knew that Mr Phineas Gow had arrived, because she heard voices in the hall, steps going up and down the grand staircase, and when she put her head out of the library door, the thumping of the baize door as it opened and shut. Something was afoot, and she knew exactly what it was.

She and Phineas Gow were to be married. He was here on a brief visit, to consolidate their agreement. To explain to her father what his prospects were. She held her breath and placed a hand at her waist. The thought of a beautiful house of her own, two carriages, a full staff, and a dress allowance with little if any restriction, made her smile. She would be comfortable, more than just comfortable, for the rest of her life. Mr Gow was a widower, and middle-aged, so his demands on her might not be too many or too onerous. She could look forward to a life of comparative leisure.

Who else was there to compare herself with than

Geraldine? Her sister had let herself in for a lifetime of looking after Denisthorn, which was not an easy estate to run. No matter how much she loved her home, its land, the village, its people, and the work that took place there, it was not an easy thing at all.

'Oh, Geraldine. What a difficult thing you are doing.' She spoke her thoughts aloud. 'Denisthorn needs so much attention and expense.' Most urgent of the tasks that her sister and Cousin Angus would have to see to, on assuming management in place of her father, would be attending to the roof. It leaked in several places and was due, overdue, for repairs and restoration. She did not envy her sister the task. The expense would be eye-watering.

Her thoughts went on to Maud Blockley, who had accepted Captain Phisgrove. In her last letter, she wrote that they had found a delightful little parsonage, which had stood empty for a number of years, and would be preparing it against the day of their wedding, which would take place after Christmas and the new year.

'We shall have a gardener and a groom for a little one-horse gig, and a cook. A girl will come in daily to attend to the usual tasks, and a laundress, every second Monday,' wrote Maude Blockley.

Athena read the letter and was happy for her friend, but was grateful she did not have to live in a *delightful little parsonage*. Athena was sure she could equal or exceed the style and standard her sister Geraldine, as a future countess, would no doubt adopt. There was no doubt that with any inheritance from old Lady Croukerne, and from her mother when it was her turn, *and* Angus's lot, Geraldine would be a wealthy woman.

She heard steps approach the library door, behind which she had hidden when Lady Croukerne went about, looking, looking looking for her. A footman opened it. 'Mr Phineas Gow, Lady Athena.' He withdrew immediately.

'Phineas, how lovely to see you again.' She noted he was already dressed for dinner, as she was. She had taken care to look her best. As the fiancée, soon wife, of such a wealthy man, she would be expected to look well turned out.

He moved quickly towards her and took both her hands. 'More than just lovely, my dear Athena. I have looked forward to this moment.'

'We do not have long before the gong.'

He kissed her tenderly, and stood back. 'I do believe you look more beautiful than the last time, in your rose garden.'

'It is my mother's, Phineas. A garden cared for exceedingly well by the gardener and his boys.'

'Very soon you will have one to rival it.'

'Really, Phineas?'

'You can have anything you want, within reason. Anything you desire.'

Her heart sang with the prospect. 'You spoil me, Phineas.'

'Well, let's see how this makes you feel.' He drew out a small but ornate leather box, opened it, and displayed to her the most beautiful diamond ring she had ever set eyes on.

'Phineas!' She placed a hand to her throat.

'Do you like it? I chose the best available jeweller,

and gave him my brief, especially with your hands in mind, and … the sparkle of your eyes.' He took her hand and slipped the ring on.

Athena could not believe the splendour of the ring. It was exactly right, both in size and style. A cluster of small diamonds surrounded a central one of exceptional size and cut. She held her hand out to admire it. 'Phineas! It's beautiful.' She parted her lips to thank him.

'I am not finished yet, my dear.' He took out another box, in which lay another ring. 'Your engagement ring, Athena, satisfies our traditions. But this second ring expresses my regard for you.'

He slipped a ring onto her right hand, and Athena looked at it in astonishment.

'Ruby,' he said, 'emerald, garnet, amethyst, ruby and diamond—they spell out *REGARD*.'

'My goodness, how clever. How thoughtful. You are so good to me. Is this not a touch extravagant, Phineas?'

'Of course it is!' he laughed. 'Of course. You deserve extravagance.'

Athena looked at both her hands. 'Thank you! Oh! There's the gong. Dinner is a little late, isn't it?'

'Well, I am glad for the delay—it has given me time to make you happy.'

'I'm overjoyed, Phineas.' Athena allowed him another kiss, and they moved towards the dining room.

Already, as she moved forward, skirt swishing and hands gleaming with rings, Athena felt that her future was assured and her dreams and plans were coming to fruition.

CHAPTER FIFTEEN

In which the honeymooners return from Venice
and
Yet another death shakes Denisthorn Hall

One of the letters in the morning post for Lady Athena was on yellowish paper. She had not had any like that for months. A number of days had passed since the evening Mr Gow had showered her with the benison of two rings. *Two* rings. The entire family had gasped. Even a visit to her grandmother at Cheltenham House had not drawn a reproof or even a mention of vulgarity.

Everyone was getting used to Athena being engaged, and being engaged to a rather wealthy man, who had promised her anything her heart desired. It was like a dream.

But the letter on the tray at breakfast made her wince. It came from Mr Alastair Updike. One of the well-penned paragraphs made her hold her breath.

> *I have heard, dear Lady Athena, although there is no announcement in the papers yet, that you and Mr Phineas Gow are engaged to be married. May I wish you every happiness. I do hope your future duties will not be an obstacle to pursuing your literary gift. You must continue to write. I dare make this presumptuous statement, having no right*

*to instruct or advise you, because your writing
is very good, and I do hope to see something
in print before too long.*

Oh, Alastair. Mr Updike was such a dear correspondent. And she did miss her quiet writing. She had no time to think of it, even during the London season—especially because of the London season—and had missed her silent hour or two of writing a day, but had missed Mr Updike and his letters more.

Hearing that he had spent some time in Normandy, and her thoughts of being left a spinster, did bring him to mind every now and then. He was a dear man, with a lively mind, who had a pleasing ability with words. They could discuss the new kind of poetry for hours, but he was not wealthy, not at all, and did not have the wherewithal to install her in a grand establishment of which she would be proud.

'I wonder if I should continue to write to him after I become Lady Gow.'

Lady Croukerne, watching her exit the dining room from the top of the stairs, descended and asked her a few questions. 'Are you talking to yourself, Athena? Has the first post arrived? Did you receive some news? Is it a London acquaintance, perhaps?'

They walked together to the day room, where sunshine slanted in through the dual aspect windows. 'Oh, look, someone has done an excellent job of the flowers today!' Lady Croukerne took her usual place and reached for the book of poetry she had left on a side table the previous day.

'It's not news, in fact, Mama. Mr Alastair Updike

has sent me his heartfelt felicitations.'

'So the news has reached places far and wide. Your father had better place an announcement. Your Grand-mama would expect us to do things properly. I shall get him to write to the papers at once.' She narrowed her eyes and craned her neck, looking at one of the windows.

Athena knew she was looking for a sighting of Frederic. 'Mama, I do believe there was a time when you wondered whether Mr Updike would speak to Papa about me.'

'But he did not, did he? Was he to be seen anywhere in London during the season?'

'No—and it's all turned out well.'

'Very well, for *you*! You will be installed at … where did you say it was?'

'Tredington. But it will take some time for the house to reach the style I desire. There are some changes I shall need to make.'

'All in good time, my dear. You have the rest of your life. No need for undue haste.' She looked out of the window again. 'What beautiful days we are having. I do declare that …'

Before her mother could say anything about her dead little brother, Athena stood and swished her skirts. 'Do you remember Sir Neville, Mama?'

Lady Croukerne swivelled her eyes towards her daughter.

'Sir Neville Robarts, the train magnate. Of course I do. Your Grand-mama rather likes him, which is surprising. Now, he is …'

Athena interrupted. 'Wealthy, and not the most handsome man we know.'

Lady Croukerne raised a hand to her lips, lest she let slip any remark about her daughter's fiancé. Her opinion of Mr Phineas Gow's visage was not any more complimentary. She thought both gentlemen to be the furthest from handsome, and the closest to ugly, any woman might think them.

'Did you not think, at some point in time, Athena, that you might have ...'

'Whether or not I was interested in Sir Neville, Mama, I should be a widow today if anything came to the fore.'

'He was knighted so young, because of his services to railway transportation in the United Kingdom. Papa did read it to us from the paper. What did you say, a *widow*? Only one thing can make you a widow!'

'It was in the paper.'

'The paper! What was in the paper? Why do you insist on reading Papa's papers?'

'They are published for everyone, Mama.'

'But ladies have other things on their minds. Other occupations.'

'A time will come when there will be women working as editors, writers, columnists and journalists. And I sincerely think that it is a time both Geraldine and myself will witness.'

'You say such improbable things, my dear. Improbable, even if ...' She held up the book of poetry. 'Even though Christina Rossetti has done well with this little book,' she remarked, as if surprised. 'Geraldine thinks women will one day wear breeches and ride mounts astride! I should think even the horses will protest. It will *never* happen.'

Athena tilted her head and allowed her mother her say. Whether or not Lady Croukerne agreed, the world would change. It had changed in the last forty years or so, and Athena could see no reason why it should not change further.

'I do believe I would be surprised too, to see Geraldine in breeches.' Her laugh was so pointed it made her mother smile too. 'But what I read today made me see that everything we think of might not come to pass, so in one respect, you are right, Mama.'

'What could I possibly be right about?' Lady Croukerne put an ironic lilt to her voice.

'Sir Neville was indeed ugly, and certainly very rich, but neither fact could keep him alive. His funeral was last Thursday in London.'

Lady Croukerne raised a hand to her lips. 'He was not an old man at all!'

'So you see, Mama—if you or Papa had tried to make a match for me with him, I should be an exceedingly young widow indeed.'

'You are so hard-hearted, daughter of mine.'

'Ha! Realistic, perhaps.'

'And the fact he was not a handsome man ...'

'... has nothing to do with anything, I agree.' Athena closed off the conversation by standing. 'I shall take a turn in the garden. Would you like to come, Mama?'

She stood on board the *Le Nord,* a steam ferry from Calais, her hat clamped firmly on her head with a steadying hand. The wind was a tremendous force, but

Geraldine was determined to stay on deck to watch the waves, the scudding clouds, and the way other passengers quickly sought companionways to get themselves below. She drew her light shawl over her hat and tied a knot. It would not sail away like that, and would protect her face from any drizzle and spume.

'I think it will be harder below,' Geraldine said to Angus, who for once was not distracted by something other than what she said. Even though the words were fairly whipped from her mouth by the stiff breeze, his head was lowered and he caught what she said.

'Yes,' he said. 'It will pitch and toss below. Here we can keep our eyes on the horizon, and look ...' he pointed. 'That line of white cliffs will eventually loom large and we shall be on home soil once more.'

'I'm glad you are as eager to return as I am, Angus.' She kept her eyes on the distant chalky line, which was hazy at best in the sea spray and light shower. The cliffs disappeared and reappeared, up and down and up, as the ship rode the waves.

'I'm afraid *holidaying*, as they call it, does not suit me. I long to be about my business. There is nothing I like better than an office, a good clerk or two, and something lucrative to get my head busy with. I do not wish to travel overseas again for quite a long time.' He took a deep breath, the wind making him cough. 'I'm afraid I shall not find a lot of time to spend at Denisthorn when we return, either. I have neglected Edinburgh enough as it is.'

Geraldine could sense it was what would happen. She nodded, asking herself how much she minded if Angus was to disappear to Scotland, leaving her to help her father with the running of the estate. She looked at the grey waves which were starting to froth and foam the further they got from Calais. There was a mighty swell, which made the ship rock.

'You seem to have good sea legs, Geraldine.'

Surprised that Angus discerned anything about her, she turned and met his eyes. 'There is a lot for us to notice about each other.'

He looked away and up. Smoke from the enormous funnel puffed, billowed, and spread above his head. It was dark heavy coal smoke that emitted from the bowels of the ship, where the furnace was fed by stokers, blackened from head to toe by their stifling blistering work. He took a moment to describe the scene below decks in the boiler room of the ship.

Geraldine was amazed he knew so much about it.

'Trains, steamships, banks, emporiums and factories—they are all businesses I understand. They all hold fascination for me, and great promise for the future. Do you not wonder what the future holds for us, Geraldine?'

This was unusually introspective of her new husband, who was usually superficial and flighty, and who had not yet spent one night in her bed. The few minutes he had lain beside her on that memorable first night meant she could look upon him as he slept, but nothing more. Geraldine did not feel different from before she married, except for the journey to Venice, which had made her confirm her love for England and for her father's estate, Denisthorn Hall.

'For us?' She made a point to strengthen her tone. 'I do wonder, but I also have confidence that it will all turn out well, Angus.'

'I am so very glad of that,' he said absently.

She could see his thoughts were turning to other things, but it was good that they at least had a moment to agree with one another.

Prudhomme looked down at the toes of her boots, wishing she had the nerve to take up her hems one inch or two. It would make her work so much lighter if her skirts were shorter. She had seen pictures of new fashions, which she could alter her clothes to imitate.

She had also seen some scandalous illustrations in a magazine that had found its way to her hands. In a spare moment, and also while seeking new ways to style Lady Croukerne's hair, she came upon two or three pictures of French women who had short fringes and sections of hair around the face cut rather short.

'What*ever* is happening to people and their modes?' she asked herself. 'Will there be a time when women lose their composure and have their hair cut short, like men?' She laughed.

It was scandalous, because short hair on women, to her mind, belonged solely in extreme illness, under a bonnet ... or in asylums.

Styling a lady's hair would, if it was shorter, prove to be much more expedient. Easier, certainly, than it was now. It took a whole day, once a month or so, to loosen Lady Croukerne's hair, free it of all the pins and ties, and give it a good wash. Rinsing and drying, towelling and combing, brushing and taming it all back into a controlled state was an exhausting task.

Her own hair no longer reached to her thighs.

Prudhomme had taken a good two feet or so off it, herself, with dressmaking shears, and she still remembered the feeling. It was like cutting flesh and blood, it was so uncommon an undertaking. And she did it in secret, pushing handfuls of hair into the compost heap out of the towel it was bunched in. But now, her tresses rolled and coiled easily into a practical bun under a small bonnet. She found it easy to control in the morning. Would the same expedient not apply to her skirts? She would have to discuss it with Mrs Beste, and show her a few pictures that would not completely shock her.

Looking after Lady Croukerne was becoming difficult for more reason than her long luxuriant hair, usually confined in two endless plaits, which took at least a quarter of an hour to coil and style each morning and each time her mistress changed dress during the day. Lady Croukerne was becoming more and more distracted with every passing day, becoming more forgetful, and mentioning her dead son more and more often.

Prudhomme looked out of a window on her way back downstairs. She had a lot to do, because she had starched a few lace fronts that morning, and they were waiting for the sadiron. But she longed for a walk out to the lake and back, along a far path where she would not be noticed from the house. Milly Fairley was always looking for company, too, and the ladies' maids generally kept together, but she wanted to avoid chatter in her mood.

A bit of fresh air, all on her own, would make her feel less repressed. She would decide whether she had enough thread to take up her black skirt, at least. A clear head would help her make that decision.

She reached the bottom of the service stairs and quickly found her way out to the courtyard, where Alice was grunting as she thumped yet another rug with the carpet beater. So she went unnoticed as she hurried along past the gate out onto the gravel and down to the path by the walled vegetable garden, where she could hear the squeaking of the gardener's wheelbarrow.

Emerging at the end of the path, she walked between the edge of the great lawn on her left and the space before the hedgerow on her right. She could hear the wind in the trees. It was a pleasant day, with warm enough sunshine. She closed her eyes and lifted her face to the light. Turning to face the house, she gazed at the bulk that was Denisthorn Hall. The great house sat comfortably on the land, its bulk nearly hiding the sun. She was so used to the way the drive down to the great gates towards the village curved outward and then in again. She knew that sight so well.

It was a peaceful afternoon, a brief pause before she had to wake her mistress from her nap so that she could give her some tea and dress her for dinner, which was taking longer and longer these days.

And there, at the end, near the gates, where the drive disappeared behind the high stone wall, there was movement. Someone was running and waving. Two figures. Prudhomme kept still and shaded her eyes. Two figures, drawing closer. One a maid, in black and white, and the other looking rather like a gardener's boy or messenger, wearing an apron. She watched them run.

The two figures crossed each other at one point, but still they ran towards her, waving, and now, she could hear their shouts. Wanting to return to the house, Prudhomme knew it was too late once they had seen her. She could see them plainly now. A maid and a messenger, and they could only be coming from one direction—Cheltenham House.

'Miss! Miss!' The maid shouted words that were more like hisses, slitting the air. '*Miss!*'

Prudhomme did not move. From behind her, two maids ran out from the courtyard, passing her, breathless, without turning to say a word. She wondered what they had seen or heard to rush out so suddenly. They must have been dallying at one of the front windows.

She took the opportunity, since someone was attending to whatever was the matter, to take two steps back, turn, and hurry back to the house.

'Her ladyship has rung for you,' someone said as soon as Prudhomme entered the servants' hall. So she ran up the stone stairs, holding onto the metal railing, her skirt held up in her right hand. Had she thought she would have peace of mind, a serene evening? She was deluded. She ran along the carpeted corridor, swiftly and silently, as long was her practice.

'Prudhomme. Something has happened. I must go down to the library at once.'

'Yes, my lady.' Very quickly, she tidied up her mistress's dress and hair, handing her a shawl.

'Thank you.'

Downstairs, Lord Croukerne sat in his wheelchair, looking up at a messenger, still in white apron over his brown clothes. 'Thank you, young man. It's not good news, but thank you. You can go back to Cheltenham House. And this time, walk—don't run. No need to run. Did you come alone?'

'Jill is waiting in the kitchen downstairs, yer ludship.'

'Both of you can have some refreshment, and then hurry along back to your house.'

'Yes, yer ludship.'

Ninian Crownrigg, Lord Croukerne, had a sad look on his face as he turned to receive his wife, who had rushed into the library.

'Has something happened, Ninian?' She did not notice that the young boy had made the mistake of passing between her and Lord Croukerne on his way out, rather than behind her.

No one noticed mistakes or faux pas when they were upset.

'Isn't that boy from Cheltenham House?'

He turned to face her. 'Mama has had a turn. She is rather unwell. Doctor Spender is there with her now. I shall order a small gig. Please do not trouble yourself.'

'Ninian!'

'Please, Edwina—there is no need for you to upset or inconvenience yourself, I said. I'll send word if it is worse than I think.' He rolled himself close to the fireplace and tugged at the bell for Thorn.

The valet was there so quickly it felt as if he had been waiting behind the door. And it was quite possible he was, because the servants were all abuzz with the news. The dowager marchioness was unwell, and all was at sixes and sevens at Cheltenham House.

Inside fifteen minutes, Lord Croukerne, his

wheelchair, his valet, his hound, Cosmo, and a groom were in a gig, jingling at a steady trot down the drive toward the village. Clouds rolled in and it looked like rain was on the way.

Passersby and villagers watched them go past, and word was already about, so people talked and gesticulated. Some said the old marchioness was of an age to expect things to happen. Others said they hoped she would recover quickly, if she had taken ill, for all the family's sake, and others predicted a time of changeability in the district.

'Unwell? How do you know she's unwell?'

'The doctor's carriage went past, about an hour ago. More than an hour.'

'She's not a spring chicken, you know.'

'But there's a wedding being planned, isn't there?'

'Is there? Up at the house? If the old countess dies they will have to kick it down the road.'

'To *what*? What are you saying?'

'To postpone it, I mean.'

'Hmm—have a bit of respect, man. These are our landed family. The entire village exists only because they are here.'

'She's a bit of a prickly old lady, though.'

'Prickly or not, her ladyship's custom is what keeps us all here.'

'I wonder what's going on behind that wall.'

Cheltenham House, or at least its gates and walls and the tops of trees in its beautiful gardens, were quite visible from the centre of the village. A knot of people stopped on the village common, to watch and wait. An umbrella or two spread as the quarter-hour ticked past.

The gig from the big house went through, and Lord Croukerne was met at the steps. Old Lady Croukerne's butler, Bann, stood to attention. A footman stepped down the stairs to help, carrying and opening a big gamp as he descended. Another came forward to take the dog's leash.

Even as he was lifted into his chair by Thorn and the groom, it was clear to the earl they had arrived too late. His mother, old Lady Croukerne, had departed this earth.

CHAPTER SIXTEEN

In which Cheltenham House falls vacant

Lady Geraldine, now properly known as Lady Crownrigg, was received in sombre tones, within a sombre atmosphere, when she returned to Denisthorn Hall from her honeymoon in Venice. Her heart sang on being home but for a few short moments. She was plunged abruptly into sadness and grief, from which she would find it hard to surface.

Herring was there, and Mrs Beste, and two of the housemaids. But the footmen were nowhere to be seen, and her mother was absent from her usual position on top of the stairs.

'Lord Croukerne is at Cheltenham House, Lady Geraldine.' It was not right that the news should reach the young mistress through anyone other than a member of the family, so Herring took two steps back, and lowered his eyes.

Angus made for the library and had poured himself a brandy before anyone else entered the room.

Geraldine divested herself of her travelling cloak and handed it to a housemaid. 'Where is Fairley? *What* is going on?' The maid bobbed a curtsey and mumbled something.

In the sitting room, she asked the same question. 'Angus, what is going on?'

'I don't know, but I expected a welcome somewhat warmer than this,' Angus muttered. He took to an armchair and looked across at his wife, who occupied a corner of a sofa.

'We can't sit here like guests, Angus. This is our home. This is our homecoming. Something momentous has happened, to cause such a big distraction, and we should inquire without delay.' She stood, turned, and saw Herring had opened the door.

'Everyone—that is, his lordship and Lady Croukerne—are at Cheltenham House, my lady.'

'Lady Croukerne too? Something's happened, Herring.' Lady Geraldine joined hands, her knuckles white, knowing the news was not good.

Angus, from the other side of the room, turned his head slightly as he poured himself another drink. 'Come on, Herring. Be the man and tell us what's up. Do we need to head down to Cheltenham House?'

'The dowager marchioness has taken ill, my lady. The message came some hours ago. Ah ... the news is not good.'

'Oh, no!' Geraldine blinked hard. 'Send to the stables for a gig for us, Herring, please. We shall hurry there to see how things are developing.'

'At once, my lady.' The butler left and closed the door.

'You can't mean to go immediately, Geraldine. You're exhausted. Our journey home was not easy.'

'Neither will be whatever we are to find at Grand-mama's house, Angus. But I'll never forgive myself if I rested rather than hastened to her side.' Geraldine asked for her cloak in the hall and was in a few seconds out on the front steps.

Angus joined her, and they waited in silence until, from the direction of the stables, a small one-horse carriage could be seen approaching. The groom driving the horse, cloth cap low above the eyes, waterproof cape gathered about the ears, and whip carefully held upright, seemed familiar.

Geraldine's eyes widened. 'Mark! Mark, I see you are still at the stables.'

'Come on, Geraldine. Let's not waste any time now that the decision to go has been made.' Angus was impatient.

Geraldine stood her ground. 'Mark! How extraordinarily ... how extraordinary to see you. I, ah— will you take us to Cheltenham House, please?'

'Without delay, my lady. We've heard the news. You'll be there in mere minutes, despite the rain.' The stable girl raised the hood over her cap.

'That groom has a strangely soft voice. How young is he? Driving a gig is not for a child, no matter how capable.' Angus settled next to Geraldine and they were off.

'Mark is an expert with horses. Soft voice or no soft voice.' Geraldine's emotions were high. Three feelings— grief, joy at the homecoming, and surprise at seeing Mary Mark again—assaulted her heart. Pulling a handkerchief from her sleeve, she dabbed at her eyes.

'Save your tears, my dear. There might be cause for more.'

'Oh, Angus. I dread to think what we should find.'

It was time to mourn again, time to reminisce, time to take stock. The dowager marchioness was no more, and despite the memory of her temper, her desire for perfection, everyone at Cheltenham House and Denisthorn Hall remarked that her absence was felt, and felt deeply.

Chief among those who missed her was naturally her son, who struggled with the loss. 'It's possibly because I am infirm now, and often think back to the days of my childhood. So it is doubly hard. I shall miss her peremptory voice, her steadfast decisions.'

'She was stern with you, a demanding mother,' Lady Croukerne observed. 'We were much more lenient with our girls.'

'If course, times were changing already when Athena and Geraldine were girls.'

'They will look fine in their black dresses, and then purple, and then lilac and grey.'

'They surely will, but that is not the chief consideration, Edwina.'

'Perhaps not, but let it not be said that we were remiss with their wardrobes. Or that of Frederic. He is outgrowing all his jackets and will soon need the attention of a tailor again.'

'Edwina, please.'

'Do not remark on the expense. It is a necessity.'

'It's not the money, Edwina, you know that.' The earl placed a hand on his forehead, tired of the irregularity of his wife's thoughts and words. What was he to do if she got worse? Perhaps if he distracted her with mention of the forthcoming wedding, she would be jolted into the here and now. 'Now, a second wedding, and so soon. After a discreet period of mourning, we can resume the plans. I am sure you have been in close conference with Mrs Jones.'

'Do you know she still calls the girls by their old nicknames? She calls them Miss Gera and Miss Anthy. Is that not the sweetest thing? Tell me, Ninian—is that not so very delightful?'

'It is surely the most endearing thought, my dear.' For once, the earl's expedient had worked, and he could send his wife down to discuss more details with the housekeeper and cook, without her being preoccupied with their dead little boy.

CHAPTER SEVENTEEN

In which the sisters resume normal life
and
Servants compare households and discuss electricity

Lady Athena stood by the window in her mother's day room at Denisthorn, breathing shallowly, considering all that had happened since her wedding to Phineas Gow. She had reason to smile, and reason to cry.

'And if you think of it,' her sister mused, talking across the room from the sofa, her face serious, 'it was long before either of our weddings that things started to go wrong.'

'It's as if you read my mind.' Athena mumbled the words. 'We are neither of us exceedingly happy since little Frederic left us.' She sighed and stroked the curtain damask. 'Too much has happened.'

'In the recent past years? Too much! You are so right. Papa's accident, two funerals, and Mama is becoming so inconsistent and forgetful. Even your presentation at court and our weddings could not lift the grey curtain which has descended on this family.'

'Surely, Geraldine, seeing the queen lifted your spirits. Surely your wedding has made you happy. Mine was postponed for so long, with the mourning period for Grand-mama. There were some weeks when I wondered when we could even *hope* to set a firm date.'

'It upset all our lives.'

'It set mine and Phineas's on its ear. We hardly knew where to turn.'

'But it took place, and you two are finally settled at Temple Grove.'

'It took too many months, but oh, it is such a lovely house! I am proceeding with my plans to make it *perfect*. All my dreams are coming true ... perhaps not all at once, but I'm making certain that the house and grounds, at least, will be at their optimal within the next two years.' Athena's eyes shone. 'Coming to visit you here at Denisthorn ...'

Geraldine hoped Athena would not make comparisons. She and Angus were busy enough not to be hurried with maintenance and improvement plans for Denisthorn Hall. 'It is so lovely to have you. Angus spends so much time in Cheltenham, because of the new bank branch, in Edinburgh because of the *old* bank branch, in London, because he says that is where *everything* happens, that I am often alone.'

'What about Maud Blockley? I mean, Maud Phisgrove, as she is now.'

'She is much more distant from me now, in what she calls her sweet little parsonage. Christmas and the new year came and went, with us in mourning, and she is now wedded too. And her letters are full of gladness. She is bursting with ... with *glee*.'

'It sounds as though she has found happiness, then.'

'As happy as one can be, with a husband forever travelling with his regiment. It can be lonely for a new wife.'

'Well, I am here at Denisthorn—with you—for a

week at least. Phineas is in Cheltenham too, for a brief stay, where he puts up at his club. He has drawn up all the papers for Angus, and a dozen or so men were employed. He says the branch will eventually run itself.'

'Run itself?'

'He says such amazing things. *Run itself!* He cannot bear to be gone from home for more than two days at a time. He loves our new home.' Athena beamed and turned slightly at the window. 'Every time I visit you I remember our wedding.' She pointed out the window. 'Do you remember how fine it all was? Do you remember the great marquee on the lawn? I was in such high spirits.'

'You looked lovely. You did. But it was reduced.' Geraldine shifted on the sofa. 'We were hardly out of mourning. Grand-mama was not there. Papa, in his horrible chair, seemed glum and mournful. Mama was distracted, and kept saying Frederic liked the bride cake!'

Athena laughed. 'And yet it was the happiest day of my life.'

'Athena, is that true?'

The older of the sisters turned. There was a beat before she answered. 'It is.' It was said quietly, as if she had just realized something.

'We are here, two sisters hardly yet married a year, in a morose mood, and yet you say you are *happy*.'

'I think it is possible, quite possible, Geraldine, to have morose moods even when, on the whole, one's life is taking a turn for the better.'

Geraldine nodded. 'It is quite strange, because before both our weddings, you were the one to speak in half-sentences, and never knew where to look!'

Athena looked amazed, and then amused. 'Well, getting married does change one, I suppose.' But she looked at her sister and deliberated. 'Does it affect all of us in the same way, I wonder? It couldn't, I suppose.'

'You have become noticeably more confident. You walk with a spring in your step. You have colour in your cheeks. You look extremely well turned out.'

'I have a whole new wardrobe. I have my own seamstress, who lives in Tredington, and who is so knowledgeable about fashions, French or otherwise. She ...'

'It is more than your wardrobe, Athena. You *glow*.'

'Glow!'

'You have taken on a different air.'

'Perhaps it is all because I have my own home, which I have always wanted. A grand home! And Phineas. He might be older by many years than Angus, but he has verve and energy and excellent humour. He is ...'

'Oh, stop, stop! There you go making comparisons again. I don't think it fair, Athena. Stop.' Geraldine rose and pulled the bell to summon someone to bring them tea. 'I think ... I think some tea will raise our spirits.'

'Where has Mama disappeared to?'

'She's taking a turn in the garden. I cannot bear to be out there with her, because she mentions our dead little brother with every breath she takes.'

'Geraldine, you used to love the outdoors.'

'Oh, believe me, I still do. It is only my daily ride ... weather permitting ... that lifts my spirits.'

'I'm so glad you still ride.'

'Of course I do! It is very nearly the only ...'

Athena raised a hand and stopped her, just as a footman opened the door.

'You rang, my lady.'

'Tea, Godwin, please. For three. Lady Croukerne will join us soon.'

'Before Mama joins us, Geraldine, please tell me what's ... something seems to be crushing your spirit. And it is too long after Grand-mama's funeral to still be grief for her.'

'A few months! Some people grieve for years. Look at Mama.'

'It's not that, I know.'

'Nothing is crushing my spirit.'

'You seem somewhat deflated. Something is on your mind. We should have a nice sisterly talk. That should go towards making you ...'

'Is that not exactly what we are doing?'

'Well, I suppose it is. We're both married women now. Our talks are not the same as when we were girls.'

'I seem to remember we had little in common. And now the only thing that makes us what you might call *the same* is the fact we are married.'

'There you are, girls!' Lady Croukerne bustled into the room, bringing with her, it seemed, great gusts of the outdoor air. She was followed closely by a housemaid pushing a trolley, so the conversation turned to the garden, and how well the gardener had pruned the rose arbour.

Fairley and Prudhomme looked at the basket of flowers between them. It lay in the little scullery where all the vases stood on shelves. There was a bucket in the sink, catching drips from the tap.

'Her ladyship brought it in.'

'Are you sure? Did she bring it down herself?'

'No, she handed it to Formby. He was in the hall. He brought it down.'

'Well, I suppose it's something. Daisies, marigolds, two roses. I could do one or two posy vases in the morning. Let's put them in water until then.'

'It's precious little, you know.'

'One of the kitchen maids will run out in the morning and get something from the gardener for the breakfast table.'

'They're all married women now. Do the young ladies still come down to breakfast?' Prudhomme looked surprised. She was always up with Lady Croukerne until eleven at least.

'Lady Geraldine does, before her morning ride. Mr Angus is away in Scotland, or London ... he is away a lot.'

'She's taking up all the slack left by his lordship's disability. He is lucky she's here. And she does everything else, because her husband is not often present.' Fairley shook her head. 'He is supposed to be learning all there is to learn to run this place. I never thought a day would come when Lady Geraldine would meet the agents in her father's library.'

'No. Not something I thought I'd see. We all thought the little baron would one day succeed. We're all lucky to have her here. She works hard and knows the estate like the back of her hand.'

'So flowers for Lady Geraldine's breakfast then.'

'Before her ride.

'Before she rides out.'

'Do you think Meg Simpson likes being at Tredington?'

'Ask her yourself. Here she comes now.'

Simpson, in a livery the other women were not used to, stopped at the door of the servants' hall. She wore a vertically striped green dress and a light green apron without a bib. She wore no bonnet, and the length of her skirt was about the ankles. 'You won't be calling me by my mistress's name now, will you?' She burst into a small laugh, covering her mouth with a hand. The other had a soiled collar in it.

'No, Meg.' Fairley smiled. 'We won't. Look at you! You might like to pop that collar of Lady Athena's into the basin. I have two of her sister's in. Soak all that starch out. We'll work on them tomorrow.'

'Thank you, Milly. Lady Gow's new wardrobe is somehow easy to look after. And because she has so much choice, nothing gets ruined through too much wear.'

'What a luxury. Tell us more.'

The ladies' maids huddled together.

'Why don't I rustle up a pot of tea? We won't be needed until an hour before the gong.' Fairley ran to the kitchen.

'I have to lay out tonight's gown.'

'And I have scarves and shawls to organize. But we can do that after a cup of tea.'

'What's it like at Tredington?'

'You're sure to find out when you visit. The house is beautiful. Not as large a house as this one, but the style, as my lady puts it, is *exquisite*.'

'Now that's a big word.'

'It suits the house! You should see the servants' quarters. We have electric light. Switches on all the door jambs. Running hot water in our bathrooms. Two for the men, two for the women. And our *housekeeper*!'

'Is she nice? Who has Lady Athena engaged?'

'Mrs Candler. And her husband is the butler! They came recommended. Their last positions were made vacant. Someone died in the city, and a house was closed down, not far from Belgrave Square.'

'Not Sir Neville's? We heard he died young.'

'Could be. So the butler and housekeeper, I heard, went from one wealthy household to another. Some people have all the luck.'

'Don't you feel isolated at Tredington? It's so distant, I hear, from anywhere.' Prudhomme was curious.

Simpson nodded thanks for the cup of tea Fairley handed her. 'Not with all the staff we have, Miss Prudhomme, and the village is close. Lovely bit of countryside. We take walks. I've made one or two friends in the girls. The cooks' assistant is a lovely girl. We have two days off a fortnight! Five footmen, an under-butler, two boots, two cooks, and all the skivvies and housemaids and kitchen maids in Warwickshire!'

'My goodness—why on earth would they need two boots?' Prudhomme's mouth formed a small pout.

'They run messages, take and send the post and newspapers, look after boots and shoes, and *they* are responsible for keeping the boot room tidy. They also do yard work. They beat the rugs, and they have tools to repair things as they come undone.'

'Like what?'

'Door knobs, the tightening of hinges, fixing boxes and stools and shelves. Everything's looked after promptly. No lamps to trim any more, but they are the ones who build the fires in the mornings.'

'What do the skivvies do then? It all sounds so modern.'

'The girls have a lot of dusting and setting straight to do. They make the beds. The housekeeper is fair, but they have a lot to do. A lot of visitors, so far. That Mrs Phisgrove is due to spend a month soon.'

'*That* Mrs Phisgrove?'

'Oh, Miss Prudhomme, I forget you are a stickler for proper behaviour.' Fairley giggled and lowered her eyes.

'Will she bring a maid? It doesn't sound like she ...'

'Oh, I don't know if she will. We have two rooms set aside, anyway,' Simpson said. 'Upstairs in the corridors, for ladies' maids and valets.'

'Goodness. The height of luxury! You don't have to share when the house is full.'

Simpson sat back. 'Lady Athena is dizzy with delight. She's still making plans for changes, even though the house looks perfect to you and me.'

'She looks joyful, it's true. I don't think I can say the same for Lady Geraldine.' Fairley looked into her cup and bit her lip. 'Oops. Telling tales out of school.'

The other two women leaned in closer.

Fairley looked at one, and then at the other. 'I've been happy, since she returned from honeymoon, where I was not allowed to go.'

'Venice would have been nice for you.'

Fairley poured herself another cup. 'Well, that's

behind us now. My lady doesn't talk about it a great deal, except for the fact she made a friend there, and is very glad for that.'

'A friend?'

'Yes, a lady from Cleeve Hill. Miss Sofia Bridwell. There are many letters from her in a week.'

'That should be good for Lady Geraldine.'

'She looks forward to her post every morning, and rides out looking rather well. I am glad for that, because Mr Angus is more often than not away from home.'

'I've heard that.'

Simpson said. 'I heard it from someone. I think he is now in Edinburgh. Does he stay at his uncle's residence when he is there?'

'How would we know? He does have property in Edinburgh. I find it hard to learn anything. His valet has a silent demeanour. It's like he is sworn to secrecy. Does not even play cards with the footmen.' Milly Fairley shook her head again. 'I do so want my mistress to be happy, because we all know it makes life a lot easier.' She leaned close again. 'But I have heard something strange.'

'What is it?' Prudhomme had one eyebrow raised, as if prepared to take what she heard with a pinch of salt.

But Simpson was curious. 'Pray tell, Milly.'

Fairley looked to either side of her. 'Keep it to yourselves, mind.'

'Of course we will.'

'I've heard my mistress call her husband *Cousin Angus*. More than just once.'

'What? They are husband and wife.'

'We all know that. But I do think she still thinks of him as a cousin, and that they are not intimate.' She squeezed her eyes shut, opened them wide again, and would say no more.

Lord Croukerne asked Thorn to wheel him to the library, where a meeting with the agents was about to take place. He positioned himself near a window and looked down at a record book, splayed open on his lap. The two men in tweed stood in front of him, both with hands clasped behind their backs.

'This looks promising, men, thank you.'

'Things have looked up, in recent weeks, my lord. We are grateful for ...' Lewis Swinnart stopped talking when the other man gave him a warning look. 'No, Lloyd, I shall say it out loud. I must admit to the fact.'

'What fact, Swinnart?' Lord Croukerne wanted to know.

It was Lloyd who spoke, Matthew Lloyd, perhaps to avoid his colleague going into diatribes of many confusing words. 'My lord, since Lady Crownrigg returned from Italy, she has been taking good interest in the running of the estate. And some of her concerns and advice have been valuable.'

'Lady Crownrigg! I doubt my daughter has ...'

'Oh, you needn't doubt for a minute, my lord, that she has the best interest of Denisthorn Hall at heart.'

'I'm sure her intentions are genuine, but her experience and her knowledge could not be.'

'She knows Denisthorn as well as either of us, sir. And I would hazard to say that her knowledge and lines of thinking are close to your own, my lord.' It was a big risk for Matthew Lloyd to take, and he knew it. His mouth was a set straight line of tension.

'Does she now?' Geraldine's father smiled and shifted in his wheelchair. He had no more to say on the subject. 'Now, men. Cheltenham House has fallen vacant since the demise of my mother, old Lady Croukerne, the dowager marchioness.'

'Yes, my lord.' Swinnart took half a step forward, noting his master too used the forbidden sobriquet. He smiled, knowing that when she was alive, the old lady much resented the fact people tended to distinguish her from Lady Edwina with the word *old*. 'We have noted a number of things, namely that the staff—or what is left of it—has been transferred here.'

'Yes. The butler and housekeeper have been pensioned off to cottages on the estate. They will live out the rest of their days in peace, that is, in grace and favour. Three of the maids are now with us, and one footman, I think. I have left it all to Herring to decide.'

'What is to become of the dowager house, my lord? Shall we now ...?'

Lord Croukerne held up a hand. 'I'll tell you what we shall do, shall I?'

Both men waited for their master to speak.

'I suggest we ask Lady Geraldine. Let's discuss it with her. I shall send her a message, consult with her, and she will be present at our next meeting.' He turned his wheelchair around, paused, and then turned back. 'And that, men, will happen whether or not Mr Crownrigg has returned from Edinburgh, or London, or Cheltenham ... or wherever he is this time.' He made a small wave and turned away again, leaving them to make their exit.

CHAPTER EIGHTEEN

In which Lady Geraldine is pleasantly surprised,
twice
and
Lady Croukerne causes a pandemonium

When she was summoned to speak to her father, Lady Geraldine looked at the footman. 'You have been back for some time now, Glover. How is your family?'

The man took a step to one side and regarded the toes of his boots. 'Very kind of you to ask, I'm sure, my lady.' He took a short breath. 'I have to say it's brilliant to be back at Denisthorn.'

She gave a lopsided smile. 'Are you being polite, or are you truly happy to be home, so to speak?'

'I returned early, my lady, because I became annoyed with constant confusion. My family does not advise me of changes that occur in my absence, and I am ...'

'... consequently more comfortable with the goings-on that occur *here*?' She seemed surprised. A great deal had happened at Denisthorn in recent years, and a lot of it was definitely confusing.

'Strangely so, ma'am. Yes. I have set duties here, and now, a room to myself.'

'As befits an under-butler.'

'Yes, my lady. Mr Herring has ...'

'... put you to much rigorous testing!' She laughed

with the man, who was no longer the young nervous boy she remembered from her childhood.

Glover held himself well, and—unlike Formby—was always neat and clean in appearance.

'And how are the new people settling in?'

'We have several new staff, my lady, as you know, and they're attempting to learn our ways and systems, as Mrs Beste calls them.'

'Things run differently here. Cheltenham House was a strict place. The housekeeper Mrs Conder and old Bann are now retired. Well, thank you, Glover.' Geraldine turned away. 'Let Lord Croukerne know I shall be down to the library in a few minutes.' She never wondered why her father wanted her. It was never taxing to exchange a few words with him. She hoped he found distraction from pain and discomfort when they conversed for a while.

He was gazing out of one of the full-length windows when she entered through the double doors. He did not turn, but looked up when she put a hand on the back of his chair. 'Papa, Glover said you would like a word.'

'I have a number of things to say. The queen is not in the best of health. She is at Osborne House still, and will stay there until she can travel back to London.'

'Queen Victoria loves the Isle of Wight, Papa.'

'Yes, and she is of venerable age. I do wonder whether we shall enter the new century with a new monarch.'

'Oh! Do not say that.'

'I know, she is well-loved.'

'Dr Spender has spoken to one of her physicians.'

He looked at the surprised look on his daughter's face. 'Hmm. I am to travel to London to see one of his assistants. They have discovered a way to treat—and perhaps cure—conditions such as mine.'

'Goodness! That would be a tremendous change for you. Do you have much hope in what they might do?'

'I have every hope, Geraldine. Even though all operations are risky, I am desperate to get out of this chair. I cannot stand it much longer.'

'So you will go to London?'

'Yes, and I shall be there for some time. Your mother will go with me, and Prudhomme, and Thorn. We are also engaging a nurse. And we shall take Ivy, the maid who came from Cheltenham House, as additional support for your mother.'

'Why Ivy?'

Lord Croukerne fidgeted with his hands. 'That girl is efficient, and she knows the ways of ladies who ... who ... who are becoming forgetful or infirm. She knows the ways of your late grandmother, and might be able to apply them to caring for your mother. Together with Prudhomme, of course.'

'I hope they work well together.'

'They are both,' Lord Croukerne said, and fidgeted again. 'They are both of amiable disposition. I see no cause to worry.' He paused. 'And there is something I need to discuss with you.'

'With me, Papa.'

'Angus is frequently away. And I admire ... I have much appreciation of his excellent efforts in banking and business. I hear he is constructing a large emporium. I don't know where, somewhere in Scotland. A large gallery, in the style of the one in Milan, which will house a number of establishments.'

'Yes, I know about it.'

'You ought to be happy, Geraldine, for his hard work and sound financial principles. He continues to establish you—and Denisthorn—against the day when he will inherit the title. I hope there will never be cause for financial concern when you inherit the estate.' He paused.

'I am happy for that, Papa.'

'Do not regret his absences.'

'I endeavour to get used to it, Papa.' She was the one to fidget with her fingers now.

'Another thing. Now that I will inherit from my mother, I shall put as much as I can into the roof, the blessed roof, so that leaks will be staved off once and for all.'

'I thought you had something good to announce. The death duties are not too onerous then.'

'They are crippling, if the truth were to be told. Sit down, my dear girl. I have something to ask of you.'

He took her hand. 'Geraldine, Cheltenham House has now fallen vacant, as you know. I find it hard to think your grandmother ... oh dear, we shall never see her again.' He put his head in his hand for a moment.

'It has not been long since she went, Papa. We are still in grey and mauve and purple.'

'She was a bit of a tyrant in her old age, but I remember her when I was a young man, and a young boy, and she was a great source of advice and comfort to me.'

'She was strong.'

'She made up in no small way for my father's … um, unreliable habits. Now, about Cheltenham House. I'm going to leave it in your hands. Prove to me they are *capable* hands, Geraldine. Look after it. See it is maintained as best you can, and tell me, what do you think we should do with it?'

Geraldine was surprised. Responsibility was being placed squarely on her shoulders. Did she like it? She would consider it later, when on her own. Her father needed a swift response. 'Yes, of course, Papa. I shall discuss it with the agents in your absence. Go to London, see your doctors, and do not worry for a second about anything here at Denisthorn.'

'Are you sure?'

'I am flattered. I'm proud that you asked me. And yes,' she said, as she rose. 'I am certain I can look after Cheltenham House.'

There was commotion in the hall, and then in the library, and then in the hall again. Maisie, Susan and Ivy were just about to exit through the baize door and make their way down to the kitchen in the morning, just after they tidied up the rooms that were used the previous evening. A footman had already removed the used glasses. Formby had carried out the ashtrays. They dusted the tables, straightened the cushions, ran the collection sweeper over the rugs, and attended to the fireplaces.

'This sweeper,' Ivy had said, 'is such a great invention. I much prefer it to the pan and brush.'

'It still needs to be emptied, and that usually falls to me,' Susan complained.

'What would you prefer, to beat the small rugs? I know, let's invent some machine to do that for us!'

'What—like the machine that toasts bread? I hear we are getting one. It runs on electricity!'

They were still talking about the inventions that were making their lives as servants easier when the fuss erupted. Quickly, very quickly, as only servants in a large household knew to be quick, the three maids slid behind the baize door, leaving it open a crack.

They peeped through, but saw precious little. Raised voices, however, gave them a hint as to what was unfolding.

'No! No, Ninian. I shall not accompany you to London!'

It was Lady Croukerne, and she sounded upset.

'Edwina, please! The servants will hear. News will travel.'

'You mean gossip. You mean *gossip*!'

Lord Croukerne's voice was not as loud as his wife's, so the maids put their ears closer to the crack.

'Whatever you choose to call it, my dear. But it will not take place if you come to London with me. Neither gossip nor news. The house in London needs your attention. You have not been to Belgrave for some time.'

'How could I possibly leave Frederic behind?' The distress in Lady Croukerne's voice was obvious.

Ivy looked at Maisie. 'Isn't the little master dead?' she whispered.

'Her ladyship doesn't think so.' She held a finger to her lips. 'Hush!'

They heard footsteps and saw that Thorn was wheeling Lord Croukerne towards the library. Cosmo's canine claws clicked on the marble tiles. Lady Croukerne followed, and silence once more descended on the front part of the house.

'Her ladyship is unhappy about going to London.'

'She will have to go, Ivy. I feel sorry for her too. She's so full of grief. She's somewhat forgetful. Even two brilliant weddings could not raise her spirits for long. Even the grand funeral for the dowager could not put it out of her mind.'

Susan pulled away from the baize door. 'And the only person who can calm her is his lordship. He knows she has to go, since she has gotten worse.' She wiped her hands down the front of her apron and took up her bucket of dusters and brushes. 'Come on, bring the sweeper down. We'd better get to dusting Mrs Beste's office and seeing to the small napkins for the wine cellar. Mr Herring asked for them last night.'

'You two do the dustin', I'll get the napkins.'

They heard shouting and protesting once more when they emerged out past the vegetable garden about twenty minutes later.

'Oh, lord. Did you leave a library window open? Ivy—did you?'

'I saw no harm. Look at this beautiful day, Maisie. If the curtains do not move, and there's not a lot of wind, leaving a window slightly open gives air to a room. The library smells of cigar smoke!'

'Yes, well ... we can hear them now. Make sure they do not see us!' Maisie seemed disconcerted. 'Their privacy is important.'

'Maisie, let me tell you something. I worked at Cheltenham House, for the old dowager, for a number of years, in and out of the village, like a stick shuttle. I know all about privacy. And open windows, what's more!'

They laughed together, but stopped when the raised voices reached them again. 'Hush!'

Lord Croukerne mumbled something.

'No! No!' Lady Croukerne's voice was low and whiny. 'Will Geraldine not go with you? Angus is always away. She will not be missed.'

'My dear,' Lord Croukerne's voice rumbled softly but clearly. 'She is needed here. Denisthorn is not to run unsupervised. I'll not have it. And I require your company in London. I am to have two operations. You will be by my side.'

'I shall, dear Ninian. I *shall* be by your side. Can we not take little Frederic along? He will be no trouble. And his nanny can travel with us.'

'Oh, Edwina ... let's discuss that once more, shall we?'

The maids moved away, giving meaningful looks to each other until they were certain they were out of earshot and not visible from the library windows. 'Let's get that basket of vegetables we were sent for.'

'I was the only one Mrs Jones sent. Are you coming too?'

They argued and gossiped all the way to the greenhouse, where the gardener waited patiently with a basket of carrots and onions. 'Is something going on at the house?' he asked.

Maisie tilted her head at him. 'Isn't there *always* something going on at Denisthorn Hall, Bert?'

'I wonder if they'll take one of you girls to London, to help with Lady Croukerne.'

Ivy cocked an eyebrow at her companions. 'His lordship has already spoken to Mrs Beste about taking me.'

'Oh, Ivy—you dark horse. When were you thinking of telling us?'

They laughed together all the way to the house.

She watched them leave from the top of the steps. The servants were ranged on the last step below her—men to her right, and women to her left. There was nearly a full complement this time; everything was settling, and would soon return to normal. The servants had all tidied themselves up and gathered for the departure, summoned by Herring, in the way they always did it at Denisthorn Hall.

Angus was to arrive the following day, which was not good timing. She would have liked her father to leave further instructions with him about the estate, about the agents, about Cheltenham House, about the hedgerows that needed laying and the tenant farmers' plans for the lambing season. And the fact some beast-drawn machinery was being replaced by steam tractors, especially to haul loads along country roads. There was so much to remember, so much to consider.

Geraldine looked as the carriages and the wagonette—which left from the side of the house—joined on the driveway and drove off together in a single file down the drive. The horses looked in excellent condition. Onward to the station they would go, and similar carriages would meet them at the London station from the Belgrave house.

The crunch of gravel was still in her ears as she turned and entered the hall. It looked like rain. Lady Croukerne had seemed calm and resigned to the journey and the long sojourn at the London house. There was no fuss before they left. But Dr Spender had visited the night before, and Geraldine suspected she might have been given some calmative for the trip. Still, the embrace she received before her mother boarded the brougham was warm and she seemed present and bright.

She had watched Prudhomme tuck a blanket around her mother's knees before the lady's maid too boarded the smaller carriage behind. It was clear to Geraldine why Miss Purl was taken along. Prudhomme was an excellent lady's maid, but Miss Purl would act as companion, to keep Lady Croukerne engaged in conversation, in walks and visits, and not allowed to descend into gloom and grief.

She took to the day sitting room to read what was left of the morning post. Later, she would see if her father had left the paper in the library. There were two invitations to open, which she propped up on the mantelpiece in there, wondering whether she felt like attending a musical soiree and an art exhibition.

'We'll see,' she said to herself. Then she saw the small envelope.

She turned it over, opened it, and was pleased to see it was from Miss Sofia Bridwell, who was writing from Cleeve Park now. So she was back from her visit to Italy. She had received more than six letters from there.

It seems problems collected and gathered like black clouds, in a large bundle, waiting for my return to England. My father has asked Sir Anthony Ross to stay, and I do think they are planning my future between them. I have no intention of sitting still for an arranged marriage. I am angry as I write this, dear Geraldine. You and your understanding nature came to mind, so I thought I would let you know of my unease, even though there is little or nothing you can do.

Geraldine put the letter down. Her new friend sounded upset, and exasperated that her father insisted on finding her a suitable husband whether she wanted to marry or not. With that family, it was not a question of doing it for the money, she suspected, but out of Sir Bernard's determination that Sofia should be married off, as all women were.

'She should refuse him,' she said aloud.

She should refuse him, whoever Sir Anthony was, if she was not comfortable with the plan. She took up the letter and moved to her desk. Noticing there was another page to Sofia's letter, she went to stand by the window to read it in good light. The day outside was greying fast, and rain seemed certain for the afternoon, which meant she would not take her ride.

'I shall ride twice as long tomorrow,' she promised herself.

I have been thinking of you. Every time I go down to our stables, or even see someone on horseback in the distance, I remember our conversations about all things to do with horses. With stables, with saddles, with these long skirts we have to wear, and how we can never hope to ride astride. We have had some good talks, and my wish is that it will not be too long before we meet again.

Geraldine quickly took up a pen, slipped a fresh sheet of paper from one of the pigeonholes in her desk, and started a reply, dipping her nib in the ink often and enjoying the writing. If her mother and father were to be away for so long in London, a visit from Sofia Bridwell during that time would not only be sensible but salutary. They would both benefit from the company. She would be diverted after days of looking at the estate books, directing the agents, reading their reports.

'We could ride together!'

She wrote a lengthy letter in support of Miss Bridwell's reluctance to be married off, and offered her company and a break from her family. 'A stay at Denisthorn Hall would be exactly what Sofia needs,' she said under her breath. 'And indeed, it would be exactly what I need, with Angus being away all the time.'

For two or three days, concerns with the house roof, two fences that had come down in a storm, a tenant who was behind with the rent, and putting up with Swinnart's long discourses to explain it all to her, Geraldine sorely needed a break.

Donning her riding habit, she regarded Fairley—after emitting two long sighs—and said it was hard work looking after Denisthorn.

'It is, my lady. It must be hard work. You do some challenging things, one of which is riding with these long heavy skirts. Did you know that there is a picture in a magazine that's come from France of a skirt that makes it all easier?'

'What's this, Fairley! How is it I have not heard of such a skirt? Are you sure it's for riding?'

'I shall bring it up directly, and leave it on your table, my lady. It's a recent issue. Mrs Beste was looking in it to find a suitable pattern for a Sunday-best jacket.'

'I should like a look as soon as you can, Fairley, and thank you.'

Geraldine took herself and her mount, Piper Chance, over hill and dale, risking being caught in yet another shower. She thought of the new foal, which was coming along so well since before her wedding. Mary Mark could not come out. She was busy mucking out stables with her father, and did not dare risk a scolding. It was many long months since they had ridden together, and she missed it acutely.

When she could see the roof of her aunt's house, Gallantrae, she knew she had come too far, and it would be dark when she got back home. Turning at a copse she knew well, she galloped downhill, and then cantered gently towards home taking a short cut over a stream.

Out of breath and happier for the ride, she gave the reins to a groom at the stables, pulled off her gloves, and hurried to the front of the house. The butler was in the hall.

'It cannot be time for the dinner gong, Herring.'

'No, my lady. The postman has been again. I was going to tray it all for you.' He took an oval silver salver and placed a stack of letters on it.

'Thank you. Oh, have you piled it all together?'

'I understand you are reading all the estate business post, my lady.'

Geraldine sighed. She sorted her private mail from the rest and took it up with her. The reply from Miss Sofia Bridwell could not make her more happy.

'Oh, what good news!' Even so, she was surprised. Pleasantly surprised that Sofia wanted to take up her offer of a visit to Denisthorn Hall so soon.

It would all work out well, and she would be able to fit in her estate duties, and enjoy the company of a guest while everyone was away. She could not have been more thankful for the acceptance.

CHAPTER NINETEEN

*In which plans are made for Cheltenham House
and
Angus Crownrigg spends an entire week at home*

It was not enough; no, not nearly enough to salve her impatience. She could not wait at the house. Geraldine ordered a gig round, donned her blue three-quarter coat, and to Herring's surprise, boarded the carriage and went to the railway station herself.

It took many hours out of a day when she should have been in her father's library adding up many rows of figures. There was an error in the accounting, and she needed to find it for herself. Balancing the books—Lord Croukerne always said—was one of the first things one learned about keeping a concern in the black.

Driving the little carriage, in a brown oilskin pulled far over her brow, was Mary Mark. They exchanged a few words and headed out in gathering gloom and chill. It was foul weather for the first half-hour, but then cleared enough for visibility to show they were approaching the station and were in good time for the train.

Geraldine stood on the platform, knowing it would be a surprise for her guest to be met by someone other than a footman from Denisthorn Hall, but this could be the establishment of a firm friendship, and she wanted it to start well.

The train steamed in and was stationary for some time before a first class carriage door opened and Miss Sofia Bridwell stepped down. She looked around, seeming confident if a bit tired, and noticed Geraldine immediately. They walked towards each other and took each other's hands.

'How wonderful and generous of you to meet me, and in this weather, too, Lady Geraldine.'

'How wonderful and generous of you to accept my invitation, Miss Bridwell. Your company is well anticipated. There will be a fire and a good tea waiting at home, I promise you. Come, we can talk in the carriage.'

And talk they did, all the way to Denisthorn Hall, where the twin fires in the hall blazed in welcome, and a fine tea was laid out in the small sitting room.

A housemaid took Miss Bridwell's cloak and hat, and she repaired to her appointed rooms before coming down, looking happy and calm.

'What a beautiful home you have, Lady Crownrigg. I am delighted with my room, whose name appears to be *Wordsworth*.' She did not mention or make excuses for the fact she came without her maid.

'My mother has given all the rooms the names of poets and authors. It is one delightful side of her. She is now in London with Papa, who is undergoing some medical interventions.'

Miss Bridwell offered auguries of success and wellbeing.

'Holly Walsh will look after you and your things while you are here. She is not fully trained as a lady's maid, so we still call her Holly. Her family is from

Manchester. But she is a lovely capable girl who pays attention to detail. I hope you find her suitable.'

'Do you know so much about each of your servants? This sounds like a caring household.'

'To achieve loyalty and hard work from a band of random persons who come here from all over the country, leaving behind their families and loved ones, it's necessary to replace what they lose with a good position and some appreciation for what they do. And they do a lot for us. It's not hard. I learn this from my father.' Geraldine had taken some time to learn it, which she did admit to Sofia Bridwell, as she went on to describe Denisthorn, and her love for her home.

'If the weather improves, we shall take a ride over the estate, even to the point of reaching Gallantrae, my aunt's house. They are Sir Herbert and Lady Fanshaw ... Athena and I call her Aunt Margery. They have a lovely establishment. I emerged to be married from under Aunt Margery's wing.'

'It must be a great comfort to your mother to have a sister so close.'

'Gallantrae was once part of the Denisthorn estate. It was sectioned off, and Aunt Margery benefited. They hold a hunt every year, and Aunt Margery runs the annual flower show. Mama likes calls from her sister, but being so close, even a long interval between visits seems not to matter.'

They partook of a substantial afternoon tea, consisting of a selection of finger sandwiches, some smoked salmon and cream cheese on croutons, petits fours, almond biscuits and an apple cake.

'You must have an excellent cook, Lady Geraldine.

This is an exceptional spread.'

'Mrs Jones is indeed wonderful, and keeps herself abreast of changing fashions in the kitchen. She loves it when we have guests, and is particularly adept at choosing petits fours.' Geraldine leaned forward. 'I do believe she is partial to showing off her skills.'

'One of which must be kitchen management—one cannot bring off a spread like this on one's own.'

Geraldine laughed. 'Since my wedding, things have changed below stairs. We have more staff than ever.'

It was two days before Sofia Bridwell confided in Geraldine about her nervousness at being 'married off'. They were riding south of Denisthorn Hall, on a part of the estate that boasted not one, but three stands of oaks with sloping meadows in between, and sprawling fields dotted with sheep, which gave them the opportunity to canter freely, and even take the occasional low jump over the stream that ran through.

They stopped close to a cluster of rocks, but could not dismount for a rest, since it was not possible to mount again without help. Below them, the countryside was dappled dark and light by the shadows of large clouds that moved slowly westward.

'You live in a fine-looking place, Lady Geraldine.'

'I think, Sofia, that we know each other well enough now to call each other by name. It would be delightful if you would.'

'Of course, Geraldine. Since our first meeting in Venice, I have known this moment would arrive. I am over the moon about this visit. If only I lived within a short ride on horseback to this marvellous spot! I am very nearly jealous.' She went on to spill her emotions, her fear of being forced into a marriage she did not want. 'Sir Anthony is forever visiting, forever trying to speak to me alone. He once had the audacity to say I was the future Lady Ross.'

'That's nerve!'

'My father contrives to leave us alone, even though he knows very well I do not want ... do not desire ... I hate the fact all women seem destined to marry, to live side-by-side with a *man*.'

Geraldine agreed. 'I remember precisely what you said to me in Venice. That you think they smell!' She turned it into a joke, but her implication was quite serious. 'You obviously could not say the same thing to your father.'

'I wish I could pack my things and run away.' Sofia wrung her gloved hands and looked out at the countryside spread below them, twisting in the saddle when her horse shifted. 'I wish I could be close enough to this scene...' She waved a hand backwards and forwards. 'It's truly magical.'

'Perhaps it looks so wonderful because of your desire to be anywhere but at Cleeve Park.'

'Perhaps.'

'You are of age, Sofia.'

'Yes, I am twenty-three. Almost an old maid.'

'And you have means of your own.'

'I have my mother's fortune. No one can touch that, she made it abundantly clear and specific in her will. She was Baron Alphandery's daughter.'

Geraldine was astonished. 'So ...'

'So it's the reason—my wealth—it's the reason Sir Anthony Ross is so interested in me. And nothing else.'

'And your father?'

'And Father cannot see why I find that so obnoxious.'

Geraldine smiled. 'Your father is also a man.'

Sofia brightened. 'You manage to say some perspicacious things while using jocular language and tone. It is a code I admire about you.'

Geraldine was quiet for two beats. 'I do not think that all women would be sympathetic to your situation. You see, I think differently, even from my sister. I realize that society manipulates women and they comply. They comply and preach the same sermon, often working against themselves. Often perpetuating what we ourselves push against.'

'Oh—how enlightening that is.'

"There are aspects about you I admire.' Geraldine returned the compliment, but she was deep in thought. 'Sofia—have you ever thought of setting up your own establishment?'

'If I were a widow it would be easy.'

'As an independent unmarried woman you could probably do it as well. I have read in the *Women's Journal* that if we lived in America, we could move from home, attend college in another county, and lead a single life ... if we had independent means, of course.'

'Geraldine, I do believe you have planted a seed in me that might grow.'

'We must discuss this carefully. Beautiful as this scene might be, it is not America!'

They turned the horses in a wide circle and made their way up and down the patchwork quilt that was that part of Gloucestershire, and reached the stables at

Denisthorn.

Mary Mark came out to take their reins and look after their horses. Her face held an uncustomary frown.

'Is everything all right, Mark?'

'Of course, your ladyship.'

It was neither the time nor the place to pursue it, so Geraldine let her inquiry drop, but the girl's unhappy face stayed on her mind. She and Sofia walked to the house slowly.

'I have an idea, Sofia. An idea you might like. I shall present it to you tonight at dinner.'

Three days of splendid weather meant Geraldine was physically rather tired, because of the time spent riding around the countryside. She had almost forgotten the magazine that Fairley had left on her table. Leafing the pages quickly, she could not see what her lady's maid had mentioned about a new fashion in riding habits. So she took the magazine down to the day room, where sun streamed in and Sofia Bridwell was already installed in a corner, with a book in her hands.

She gazed absentmindedly out of a window. 'I am reading what George Sand had to say about the institution of marriage,' Geraldine's guest said, with a pert smile.

'George Sand. Let me try and remember ...'

'George Sand is the name chosen by a female writer, who put out quite an astonishing body of work, which includes dozens of novels. But this is a collection of essays—which I found in your library—which contains one of her works.'

'Is she not very complimentary about marriage?'

'Not at all. Even though she married herself, and had two children, I think, she did not—at least in this piece—find much to say that is positive.' She placed a bookmark between the pages and put the book down. 'I thought long and hard about what you proposed last night at dinner, Geraldine.'

'Oh, I am so happy that you gave it some consideration.'

'I asked so many questions!'

'As was right and reasonable.'

'Do you need no advice or approval from Lord Croukerne?'

'No.'

'Or from your husband, Geraldine?'

'No. Angus is not yet in charge of the estate.' Geraldine seemed quite firm about her idea. 'And father said quite explicitly that I was to look after Cheltenham House, and that he trusts my judgement.'

'When you offered me a permanent tenancy, I was so astonished that I must not have paid enough attention to the exquisite salmon.'

'Oh, good salmon is one of Cook's specialties. And we often enjoy it here. But the opportunity to help a friend—because I think of you now as a dear friend, Sofia—does not come up as often.'

'Would you consider me—a woman on her own— an appropriate resident for Cheltenham House?'

'Without question.'

'I have thought of Sir Anthony, and what life might be like, married to him. And reading George Sand has strengthened my determination to refuse him.'

'What did George Sand write?'

'Many things, but salient among them is this.' Sofia put her hand on the book she had just placed on the sofa beside her. *'No human creature can give orders to love,* she wrote. And since I think the only kind of marriage that makes sense is one based on love, I cannot simply marry because custom and society demand I should. My father cannot order me to love Sir Anthony.'

'Indeed he cannot.' Geraldine paused and thought about her own marriage.

Did she love Angus? She knew the answer. She loved Denisthorn more, and did hope that love between herself and Angus would develop with time.

'Love is a difficult emotion to quantify,' she said. 'But as far as being a woman on your own is concerned, I consider you a woman of independent means who can do as she pleases. You can have Cheltenham House as your establishment. And I should be delighted to help you set it all up. Papa will be pleased to see it occupied and maintained.'

'Do you know how happy it will make me?'

'I don't think you can know that yourself yet!' Geraldine laughed. 'Perhaps deciding in at least a year would be appropriate. We ought to take a look straight away.' She moved to the bell to ring for a footman. 'Now Grand-mama kept only one carriage and stabled her horse at the public house. You might want a carriage horse and a decent mount—or two—so I suggest we think of looking at the old stables and fitting them out properly.'

'How marvellous! It will be a dream come true.'

'Before we make more plans, we should take a

proper look.'

A footman opened the door.

'Ah, there you are, Formby. Please send down to the stables for the small brougham to Cheltenham House.'

'Yes, my lady, right away.'

Geraldine turned to the magazine. 'Look at what Fairley brought up for me, Sofia. A magazine with an illustration of the new riding habits. They illustrate what they call *The Safety Skirt*.'

Sofia leaned forward to have a good look.

'They're breeches! Breeches with a panel to hide them, on the front, and perhaps buttons down the side. Oh, how convenient. Can you imagine the comfort? They are breeches, and one need no longer fear the danger of falling and being dragged along by tangled skirts, drawers to the sky, attached to a spooked mount and courting injury or death! This is genius.'

Geraldine laughed at her friend's description of what a fall might be like. Neither of them had been dragged in that manner, but she was sure every female rider perched on a side saddle feared it.

They examined the pictures and descriptions together. What Sofia said was true. It was a simple expedient to tailor riding trousers covered by a single layered skirt, with a free seam that allowed movement and comfort.

'Do you think what I think, Sofia?'

The young woman looked up. 'Yes. I think I do. It is not a step too far to think of us riding astride a horse in a few years.'

Geraldine—for fear of shocking her friend—did

not mention that she had, on more than one occasion, donned male apparel and ridden astride in the company of Mary Mark. She would leave that revelation for when she and Sofia became more intimate friends.

They drove out to Cheltenham House, this time with a groom at the reins. He stood to attention and helped the ladies board the small carriage with one hand.

'Where is Mark?' Geraldine was curious, because Mary Mark often drove her around.

'Mr Mark, the stable master, yer ladyship, is seeing to settling the feed in t'barn. We've managed to trap a number of mice. I mean ... of vermin, ma'am.'

'I mean Mary Mark. I hope she is not unwell.'

'Mary Mark does not drive carriages, my lady.'

Geraldine laughed and looked away. 'Of course not. No. A girl could not, could she? She must be mucking out the stalls, carrying buckets and pushing a barrow.'

'Her father wants her to seek a position in a house, my lady. That is what ...' He stopped. 'I beg yer pardon, my lady.

'You're not being indiscreet, young man. Go on.'

'She's bein' directed to seek a maid's position, she said to me. And she ... she doesn't want to work indoors.' The boy raised a hand to his mouth, as if he regretted the words, as if he had said too much.

They got to Cheltenham House just as the sun was striking the front windowpanes before it got low behind the trees opposite.

'Oh! It's *lovely*. And much larger than you

described, Geraldine.' Sofia held up both hands, her delight showing in her face.

'It is about a quarter the size of Denisthorn, but elegant, and more or less well kept. The gardens are its paramount feature. Grand-mama loved the gardens. The house is laid out conveniently, and it's been wired. The whole village is getting electricity. We are now starting to wonder how anybody did anything after dark, before we had wired light. Papa saw to it for Cheltenham House when my grandmother moved here. The old earl, my grandfather, had passed away, and he had inherited, so he made sure his mother was comfortable.'

'How modern.'

'I don't know much about it, but Papa says the generator is splendid! He is superlatively proud of the Electric Light Act, he calls it, which will take the darkness away from all people soon.'

Sofia acknowledged what her friend said, but was fascinated by the aspect of the house. 'Are you sure you want a tenant in this charming residence?'

Geraldine turned and regarded the lady, who was not many more than two years her senior, with a frank look in her eyes. 'It won't be so much a tenant as a friend, Sofia. I have seen the kind of person you are, and how you jealously guard your life, your person ... your singularity.'

'My singularity.' She whispered it under her breath. 'Indeed.' Her mouth made a straight line as they made their way up the front concourse, not as long as its grand name suggested.

Geraldine jangled a bunch of keys. 'The house is completely shut down. There are probably dust sheets everywhere. The housekeeper and butler have been pensioned off. They now live in an estate cottage, but ...'

'Let's just have a look. I don't think you will appreciate how angry my father will be.' Sofia teetered between joy and confidence, and hesitation and anxiety.

Geraldine gave her a questioning glance. 'Does he not want the best for you?'

'I am his only daughter. My brother Roger died when he was fourteen, the same day as my mother. Their carriage left the road and everyone perished down a steep precipice. Not even the horses survived.'

'I am so sorry to hear that.'

'So he expects me to give him grandchildren. To marry well and give our house a master, after he is gone.'

'Do you feel it is your responsibility?'

'You might understand better than others.' Sofia stopped at the top of the stairs while Geraldine sought the right key.

'You know—this door is probably barred on the inside. We need to find the service door past the courtyard. Why do you think I understand?'

They walked around the house, past a small gate, into a courtyard, where crates, baskets and barrows still stood. 'This is the key, I am sure,' Geraldine said.

'Haven't you done much the same thing I mentioned? You have married the heir to give Denisthorn a master.'

Geraldine knew Sofia watched her hold her breath. For an instant, all that could be heard was the wind picking up through the trees behind them.

'I did it for special reasons. I ... I did. Angus is a nice man. I love Denisthorn too much to be parted from it. I did nothing to encourage his proposal. If Athena had accepted him, she would be in my place now. Angus would be at Denisthorn whatever happened. He inherits the title. I could not bear to think of some stranger, an unknown woman, take charge of my home. He is the heir. There is nothing anyone can do about that.'

'I see.'

'Athena wanted to wait for someone fantastically wealthy. Angus was never enough for her. He's not a poor man by any means. But she wanted more.'

'I see. I am so sorry I spoke out of turn.'

Geraldine twisted a second key and the service door opened. They walked into the corridor to the kitchen, the servants' sitting room, and the small nook used by the cook and housekeeper. 'You did not. It was not out of turn. I think that's what it must look like to all the world. It looks like I married Angus to give Denisthorn a master. Papa too thinks that. But I married Angus to keep Denisthorn to *myself*.'

They stepped up the stairs and found an arched baize door. 'Here we are—see for yourself, Sofia.'

The telegram hung from Geraldine's hand after she slipped it off the salver held by Godwin. They had just completed the sweet course, in the dining room at Denisthorn.

'It arrived just now, my lady.'

'Thank you.' She looked at it for a long time. It was from Angus. His message, when she tore it open, said he would be arriving in the morning.

'So, the fates have decided that you will renew your

acquaintance with my husband. He will be here in the morning,' she said to Sofia at dinner. 'I have had a telegram.'

They were both tired but happy after their visit to Cheltenham House, and Sofia was rather close to committing to a tenancy there.

The door opened and Herring entered with a salver. 'My lady.'

'Another telegram!'

This time, it was from Lord Croukerne. 'Oh! It is from Papa in London.' She did not disclose the content to her friend, instead reading it silently, and giving a faint smile.

> *Main operation is in the morning STOP I shall*
> *telegraph results if able STOP Thinking of you*
> *darling Geraldine STOP*

'It is good to hear from him, and that he is well and hopeful,' she said to her guest, guessing a similar telegram would have made its way to Athena at Tredington. He was a dutiful father. 'Would you like to adjourn to the drawing room? Godwin will pour us both a brandy.'

Geraldine did not know how to feel. And she said so, after steadying herself with a sip or two of brandy. 'Angus spends so little time by my side I have not yet ah ... deciphered the true meaning of being married. There are moments when I feel I am a more mature woman, and others when I feel utterly unchanged from a year ago. '

Sofia Bridwell raised a finger. 'I dare not offer you

advice, not being married myself, but a word of comfort seems to be in order. I saw your face when you read your husband's telegram, and I am known to be an observant person.'

'I noticed that in Venice,' Geraldine laughed. 'You also seem to retain new knowledge in an efficient way. Your memory for detail is excellent.'

'Thank you, dear Geraldine. Let me point out one thing that might assuage your confusion. What I noted here is that you have the best of both worlds. Never take that for granted. You have retained your beloved Denisthorn, you are married, therefore satisfying most social requisites. It is plain the servants acknowledge your position. And you are often alone, which is probably the envy of a lot of married women, who quickly tire of their husbands' ways at home.'

Geraldine's eyes grew wide. 'Is that a fact?'

'Oh, yes! I had occasion to listen to the conversations of a number of married women, both in Venice and elsewhere. Not all are happy. Not all are besotted by their husbands' habits. Men stay free, you see. Free to do much what they choose. And some say the happiness dissolves with time. The men cease to treat them in the same way as when they pursued them as young girls.'

'In what way?'

'The favours stop, the loving ways stop, the frequent letters stop, as do the gifts and most of the attention.'

'Goodness.'

'Some of them say their attention turns to someone else.'

'Someone else!'

'Yes, another woman. So the wives either ignore the changed behaviour, and take it as their lot, or they protest and make a fuss. The latter does not work in their favour. Society always gives the benefit of the doubt—any doubt—to a man.'

Her husband was in a charming mood, sitting with his wife and her guest for an hour or so each evening. He took tours of the estate with the agents, listening to their reports and advice. He even visited the servants' hall to pay his respects, which was a great surprise. Angus Crownrigg appeared to be turning into a dutiful master and attentive husband. Geraldine did not question the change she saw in him.

At dinner on the third day, Geraldine turned to Angus and remarked about the tastiness of the duck they were eating.

'It is certainly better than anything we partook of in Venice,' he laughed. 'And served in the manner to which we are accustomed.'

'I have decided what to do with Cheltenham House, Angus.' She looked out and up and caught a look from Sofia, who put her fork and knife down. A footman took away her plate.

'*You* decided what to do!' Angus held his fork in the air, then lowered it slowly.

'Yes, I did. Papa gave me responsibility for the house just before he left for London. He feels I am always present here, and capable of making decisions about it.' She gazed confidently at him, a subtle smile on her lips.

'He is confident I can see to its on-going maintenance and use.'

'Well ... I ... in that case. I suppose it's one thing about which—in the future—I should not have to trouble myself.'

'Indeed. It will be off your desk.'

'What a modern expression, Geraldine.'

'We are nothing if not modern women, are we not, Sofia?' She addressed her friend with a broader smile.

'I suppose.' Angus returned his attention to the duck on his plate.

There was silence from Sofia Bridwell, who fidgeted with the napkin on her lap.

'Sofia has accepted to take up tenancy at Cheltenham House. She will be our neighbour.'

Angus Crownrigg was rendered speechless. He looked at his wife as though she had said something completely mad. 'Miss Bridwell! A tenant? *A tenancy?* How will that ...?' He looked from his wife's face to Sofia's, and back again. 'I see developments have happened in my absence.'

'Oh,' Geraldine gave a dismissive wave, to indicate it was nothing untoward. 'You will also have found, speaking to the agents, that everything has run more or less like clockwork in your absence, Angus. Repairs, maintenance, staff, harvests ... very little has gone amiss on the estate, not even with the lambing, which could not be remedied almost immediately. They came to consult with me. There is even a new farrier's apprentice. This, you might find, relieves you of a number of worries.'

'Does that not please you enormously, Mr

Crownrigg?' Sofia's soft voice pulled the man to the here and now at that table.

He nodded, put down his fork and knife, and heaved a tempered sigh. 'Did you really interview a new farrier?'

Geraldine laughed. 'All interrogations and tests were done by Ford, the old retainer. He is more than pleased with the new man.'

'You are quite *en courant* of the matters to do with the stables, and the estate in general, I suppose, Geraldine. It requires ... I mean it needs ... that is, it is nothing if not good news. Cousin Ninian will be pleased.'

Geraldine saw he realized before saying anything else that he was not yet the heir. 'Papa cannot be troubled while he is in London this time. Medical interventions require peace. He needs to be free of worries and concern about Denisthorn.'

'Indeed.' Angus curved his lips in an obviously formal smile to each of the ladies. 'Would you like to withdraw, ladies? I am going to smoke a cigar and think, over some brandy.'

'We shall, after the sweet course.'

'Ah, yes, yes—of course.'

That night, there was a soft knock on Geraldine's bedroom door. Fairley had left a good ten minutes before, and the house had fallen quiet.

'My dear?' Angus put his head in and looked to see whether Geraldine was already in bed.

She sat, wearing a nightgown edged in Venetian lace, on the edge of the counterpane, which had been folded down by the careful lady's maid. 'Angus.'

He came and sat beside her, curling his left arm around her shoulders. 'My darling, I have been neglecting you.'

'I do not feel that in the slightest, Angus. As a matter of ...'

He took her chin in his hand and kissed Geraldine on the lips, a long kiss which would have made her struggle if she did not think quickly.

Here it was; what marriage was about. At last, the intimate part that had not yet happened, which she wondered about. It was sudden and unexpected, and yet it was not.

He did not speak much, except to mumble the words *darling* and *sweetness* and *my lovely*. They were terms of endearment she had not heard from him, ever. Perhaps they were words that only accompanied this intimacy. Perhaps they were the 'bedroom words' she had read about in a novel.

Her mind filled with those words, jumbled together, and more words, and still more, until the confusion in her head settled, and she realized it was over. He turned away, and she rearranged her nightgown, reddening as she pulled and pulled until her knees were covered.

'What you do now, darling,' he said in a normal voice, 'is use the washstand to uh ... tidy yourself up. You know.'

'The washstand?'

'Look after yourself, Geraldine.'

She gave a small exclamation of surprise. '*Ah*. The ... the bathroom, then.'

She detected a small change in her eyes when she regarded her face in the mirror. But what she saw, which immediately cleared itself in her mind, was the reason why her husband's intimate approach happened that night. Angus Crownrigg, after what he was told at table about her management of the estate, was asserting his hold, his domain over his wife. It was not something she could discuss with anyone, but Geraldine felt it. She felt it very strongly.

When she returned, having paused for a moment to peer in the dressing table mirror to see whether she detected the changes someone said would appear in her entire demeanour, Angus was sprawled on the left side of the bed, fast asleep.

He visited her three nights during the week he was there, and for three nights she studied herself in the mirror, detecting subtle differences. There was a little something of what people might have meant.

Saying nothing to Sofia Bridwell, she did not know whether to confide in another woman or not, deciding to hint to Athena, when they next met, since she was the closest young married woman in her circle of acquaintance.

'My sister will know,' she said to the mirror. 'Won't she?'

The heir to the title, the heir to Denisthorn Hall, left in a flurry of carriage and bags and boxes, with two footmen strapping the luggage to the back of the brougham and most of the household lined up for his departure.

'I feel like a guest, Geraldine. Perhaps we can dispense with formality, seeing I go away and return so often.'

'Perhaps, Angus.'

He noticed Sofia Bridwell did not stand on the steps. As a guest, she had the option to stay upstairs. 'How long will Miss Bridwell stay on?'

'I am enjoying her stay immensely, Angus, and we have plans to make.'

'So that her move here, to Cheltenham House, will go smoothly, and without incident. Yes, I see that. What have her people said, if anything?'

'I do not think she has told them yet.'

'Right. Well, I am ready to set off. Goodbye, my dear.'

CHAPTER TWENTY

In which the Denisthorn staff gets a shake up
and
The sisters have an intimate conversation

When Mrs Beste summoned a servant to her office, it was often to give a reproach or warning. All the female maids and skivvies knew that compliments and praise were not meted out lavishly. But they did occur, since both the housekeeper and cook were fair women who appreciated hard work, tasks executed and finished properly, and effort.

Holly Walsh stood on the rug in front of the housekeeper's desk with her hands clasped behind her back. 'You sent for me, Mrs Beste.'

The housekeeper saw the look of unease on the maid's face. 'Yes, Holly. As you know, we now have three uniformed housemaids at Denisthorn. And we are soon to have a fourth. I find that excessive.'

The maid's face dropped. She held her breath, not uttering a single word.

'I see you are allowing me to finish before you speak.'

'Mrs Beste, I have no idea what you are about to say.' She tried to put the words out without emotion, but her voice broke.

'Don't worry. The news is not bad. On the contrary, I think you will like the latest development. But

I must ask you one thing before I tell you what Mr Herring and I are planning. Will you do me—and yourself—the favour of keeping these developments to yourself?'

Holly Walsh shifted her feet. Her uneasiness was making her nervous, but she managed to nod. 'Of course, Mrs Beste.'

'Promise me. Promise, Holly, because if word gets out it will upset the applecart.'

'The applecart. Good. I mean, fine. I mean ... that won't do. I won't say a word to anyone.'

'So go now, and return tomorrow after dinner has been cleared away, and after you have looked after our guest, Miss Bridwell, and we can discuss what has been proposed. Miss Bridwell will be here another few days, so make sure she is comfortable and lacks nothing. Is that clear?'

The maid bobbed a token curtsey and took herself out of the office, stopping after closing the door behind her to take a deep breath. 'Oh goodness me, goodness me. What on earth have they got in store for me?'

She looked at her boots, her cuffs, her apron. She liked her position and did not wish to lose it, so she supposed that whatever the *developments* were, she was bound to do what she was told.

Mrs Beste sighed and sat back behind her desk, deciding that all these little talks with the staff were exhausting, and she required a powder, a cup of tea, and a lie down. She did not like disrupting the smooth workings of Denisthorn Hall, below stairs. But she had received instructions, and there were no alternatives to doing exactly what she was told.

At Tredington, all was sweetness and light. Athena put aside a number of swatches and samples, catalogues and written quotations, and felt it was time for a tray.

Ringing for a servant, she touched the mantelpiece and wondered whether Carrara marble would look nice for the fireplaces, or whether a black *Pietra Dura* surround for each hearth would endure better into the future.

She was thoroughly enjoying making her new establishment fairly sparkle with new style. But what she appreciated more than anything else—and it was a new feeling for her—was the attention and generosity of Phineas, who was never short of praise, and offered genuine remarks when she asked if he liked something.

'One of the hardest things I have found, Phineas ...'

'What is that, dear Athena? I hope nothing is *too* hard.'

She looked into his eyes, the more pleasing feature of his face, because they looked out sweetly and placidly on a world that presented him with problems with every passing day, in his role as barrister. The man stayed pleasant and calm, and never erupted into impatience or anger.

'I find it testing to remember the servants' names! There are so many.'

'We might find that attrition will look after that little problem. There are methods that aid the memory, you know.'

'Are there?'

He sat next to her on the sofa, nodded at the maid who came in with a tray, as if she could read her mistress's thoughts, and took her hand when the door had closed firmly behind her. 'That was Jane. We have two Janes. One is small and tidy, with a button nose. The other has reddish apple cheeks, and speaks with a broad Yorkshire accent.'

He spent the next fifteen minutes or so pouring his wife tea, offering her little cakes, and showing her ways to remember who of their footmen was who. He made her laugh, and taught her the principles of what he called *mnemonics*.

'You are so observant and clever, Phineas.'

'In my line, one has to be. Success depends on scrutiny.'

'You are so good and patient with me.'

'Special, special, because it's for you.' He released her hand and went to pull aside a curtain. 'We seem to get on tremendously well. You are good and patient, too.' He held up a finger. 'We had a superlative honeymoon, and have returned to real life, yet we are still discovering things about each other.'

'Some people say it takes a year or two.'

'Athena, my dearest.' He drew closer, sat by her side again, and took her face between his hands, kissing her on the forehead. 'It is my fondest wish that the stage we are in, and the feelings I see developing, will last us well into our marriage, which is still like a dream to me.'

'You say such nice things, Phineas.'

'They are all true, my dearest love.'

'So will it disrupt our happiness,' she asked, tongue slightly in cheek, 'if I say Geraldine is coming to spend four days with us?'

The man stood and raised his arms. He looked

better, leaner, since his wedding, and something had given him an air that did not completely rejuvenate his aspect, but certainly gave him a more pleasant stance. 'Of course not! What an excellent coincidence—I have a clerk coming for three days to write up some deeds. But, Athena, your sister is *always* welcome. It will be lovely for you. I shall make sure you have ample time to converse. I hope the weather is fine enough to take one or two of our famous walks.' He seemed delighted.

And Athena knew he was. 'Thank you, Phineas.'

'It's a good thing I have this difficult case coming up in Cheltenham. I will be ensconced in my office buried in papers, and will be making frequent trips to and from chambers. You and Geraldine will have few interruptions. And if she wishes to ride while she is here ...'

'You remember everything, Phineas.'

He laughed. 'If only that were true.'

Athena stressed the fact. 'You do.'

'If it has anything at all to do with you and your family, I think I have reason to pay attention, my love. Geraldine will find there is a suitable mount in the stables.'

'But ...'

'I have acquired two nice mares against the day. And you did hire a new groom.'

'I did.'

'There you go, then. We are all ready to receive her. And perhaps her visit will coincide with Mrs Phisgrove's?'

He did remember everything. Athena considered herself quite fortunate to receive such attention about her affairs. 'Only for one day's overlap. It will be wonderful to see Maud again.' She made to take up a catalogue.

'Leave that for now, Athena, there's something I forgot to say. You might like this. I have ordered you a handsome *bonheur du jour*, in ebonised mahogany. You must have somewhere special to do your writing.'

'Phineas—how thoughtful. I do want to set time aside for writing. A new desk would be perfect!'

'I know. I chose the style to go with what you have done in your day sitting room. Now, join me on a walk. I have looked out of the window and see the afternoon is clear and windless. Let me get your shawl.'

They walked off the delicious tea of which they had partaken, and strolled arm in arm to the postern gate, which was about ten minutes from the back of the house. It trailed with ivy, which tangled through the pickets and posts.

'Och, aye. Now that is pretty, my dear.'

'We have such a wonderful home, Phineas. It is all exceptionally pretty at this time of year. I shall advise a gardener, though, to see to the ivy, lest it becomes impossible to open this gate. Now that we have enjoyed how it looks, we can have it tidied up.'

'I like the way you think.'

Unbeknownst to them, Athena and Phineas were watched from the gate of the service courtyard. A footman drawing at a clay pipe, and a housemaid in black and white livery, who tapped her companion's elbow for the occasional puff, stood there, enjoying the still air.

'If the wind rises we can expect rain,' she said. 'I feel it in my waters.'

'P'rhaps those clouds o'er the woods are a better forecaster than yer waters, Jane.'

'Ye know what I can forecast, that needs neither clouds nor waters, Jack Oxnard?'

He saw her looking out toward the postern gate, indicating their master and his wife with her chin. 'They be close as close.' She crossed fingers of both hands. 'Close as these fingers, they be.'

'Newly married.'

'Ah—more than just that. They're ... what's that word cook uses all the time? They are an *exception*, like quail eggs that last until July.'

'Quail eggs are all gone by mid-June.'

'That's what I'm sayin'. They're an *exception*.' She waggled a finger in the direction of the distant gate. 'That's love, is what I call it, Jack.'

'Huh! Rare. Rare to have it last, unless it finds an obstacle. That's when love lasts, when it's got something in its way.'

She noted his irony. 'Is that a bit of bitterness I hear?' She laughed again. 'It might be rare, but we have it right here at Temple Grove, and ...' She pointed again. 'I predict the arrival of some small Gows afore too long.'

'That'll cut out more work for you girls, won't it?'

'Everything cuts out work for us girls, Jack. Everything that happens in gentlefolks' houses.'

Mr Herring and Mrs Beste had regular meetings.

Equipped with pencils and notebooks, they carefully recorded, made lists, found points to discuss, and put tasks against the names of members of Denisthorn Hall staff most likely to carry a job out properly, and to its satisfying conclusion.

But some jobs were never completed.

Mr Herring rubbed the back of his writing hand and stopped, capping his favourite fountain pen and slipping it into his breast pocket. 'Do you remember me reading you a bit of news a while back, Mrs Beste?'

'You read or remark about news regularly, Mr Herring.'

'But think back now,' he counted on his fingers. 'Oh, it's longer ago than I thought. My goodness, it's more than seven years. Eight, even.'

'Time flies. And we will age and be pensioned off to a couple of cottages, just like Bann and Mrs Cooper from Cheltenham House. But what were you going to remind me of?'

'The Firth of Forth, Scotland, and the bridge that spans it.'

'Ah! Quite a bridge, that is.'

'So you remember.'

'When it opened, you showed me a drawing of it in the newspaper. Extremely strange shape, rather modern. It was a big picture ... because it is a *long* bridge.'

'With complicated girders. And running this house, for you and me, Mrs Beste, is like painting that very bridge.' His deep voice, surprising in a man so lean, boomed in the small space.

'Painting the Firth of Forth Bridge!'

'Painting the bridge. The instant you reach the

end, and you think it's over, you must start all over again since the starting end now needs attention, because it takes so long.' He smiled at his clever observation. 'It's a never-ending task.'

'Indeed. We thought it would all be lighter and more practical when the young ladies got married. But we now have more servants than ever, more to do, and with his lordship come back from London requiring special care, and a nurse staying up where the nursery used to be, it's very busy.' Mrs Beste tapped her pencil against the cover of her book.

Mr Herring stroked the cover of his.

In the silence that ensued, the babble of voices from the servants' hall reached them.

'The first sitting is there.' The housekeeper looked at the clock on the butler's office wall. 'We'd better attend to things. I'll send you in a tray, if you like.'

'No need to trouble yourself. Please sit for a moment more—we can both make the second sitting in half an hour. Miss Pridwell is moving in soon, down the road—Cheltenham House will go through some changes.'

'Good ones, Mr Herring, good ones. She's a nice lady, as we've seen when she was here. Good company for our Lady Geraldine.'

'Without a doubt. But new arrangements always bring a few disruptions. They make waves. So ... Holly Walsh will move there, to be a housemaid, because Miss Pridwell brings her own lady's maid, and a companion, who used to be her governess.'

'Oh, no. No, Mr Herring. There is a bit of doubt as to whether that will happen. Her ladyship has suggested that she does not know if any servants will be coming. I'm not sure at all about the companion. What else have you got in that book of yours?'

'Oh dear, oh dear. Another problem. You're going to have to think about Holly Walsh and her duties, then.'

'I'm considering a number of aspects we have to address. What else is in your book?'

He smiled. 'Lady Geraldine has made a specific request on behalf of Miss Bridwell. I must speak to the head groom. She wants—of all people—Mr Mark's daughter to be her gardener at Cheltenham House! Gardener and head groom. A *woman*.'

'Are you sure? What happened to old Lady Croukerne's gardener?'

'Oh, he's gone off to work on some grand estate near Windsor.' The butler shook his head in disbelief.

'Climbing high in the world, eh—like his roses.'

'I don't think we can gainsay the new mistress of that house.'

'Quite right, not for us to contradict. Ivy won't be going back, will she? She's only been with us a short while.'

'I shall ask Lady Geraldine, but it would also be helpful to ask Ivy herself, because her ladyship will no doubt ask whether Ivy is agreeable to the plan, and I want to have a ready answer.'

'We should be doing all this planning with Lady Croukerne. It's sad that we cannot.'

'I cannot tell you how sad it makes me too, that she has become so forgetful. She cannot even recall being in London as recently as a month or two ago. And yet ... and yet she can remember perfectly how the little baron liked his eggs.'

'Right.' The butler stood. 'Do let her know what's going on, though. Tell her Lady Geraldine is perfectly capable of running the house business. We should need to discuss all this once more when it becomes firm. When is Miss Pridwell coming for good?'

'There was trouble at her father's house.'

'Is that gossip, Mrs Beste?'

'You know that does not happen at Denisthorn.'

'Hmm.' The butler blinked. The ironic saying left his lips. 'There are no secrets at Denisthorn Hall.'

'I don't know …' Mrs Beste shrugged.

'It would not do to dwell on gossip. Nothing is accurate until it is confirmed or decisively acknowledged by the people concerned themselves.'

'Yes, Mr Herring.'

'Very good, then.'

Lady Geraldine Crownrigg stood still in the front concourse of her sister's mansion outside Tredington, a long half-hour in the brougham from the station in Cheltenham. Her face was a mask of pure astonishment. 'Athena, you are outdoing yourself. This is a magnificent house. Look at the grounds! You also have a small mirror lake.'

'How could I resist? I like the one at Denisthorn so much.'

'Do you? Now that is a new disclosure.'

'One does not know how much they like something until they cannot look at it every day! But Geraldine—the lake is not as large as it looks. It's an optical illusion! It took a fortnight to dig out, a week to fill, and a further week to landscape properly. You would think, because of the fuss that was made by the groundsmen, that Capability Brown himself was designing the thing!'

'Considering he died more than a hundred years ago ...'

'Oh, you precise thing! Since when have you added accuracy to your quiver of arrows?'

'I can *accurately* say that you are setting yourself up rather well, here at Temple Grove.' Geraldine was going to add that when one married for money, one should not be surprised when one's surroundings are splendid. But she held the words in and exclaimed at the wondrous herbaceous borders.

CHAPTER TWENTY-ONE

In which Mary Mark makes two startling revelations
and
Differences in households become apparent

Geraldine had completely forgotten that her Grand-mama had often stated there was a distinct draught in the room she had allotted to Miss Bridwell during her stay at Denisthorn.

'Are you sure your room is not draughty, Sofia? I regret giving you Wordsworth now, when I remember how my grandmother disliked the room.'

'It is perfectly comfortable. I have detected no draught.'

'Please tell me if you do. I should have given you Keats, but that room has a bad reputation.'

Sofia laughed. 'Does it? Pray tell me what happened there. It sounds like a rollicking family anecdote.'

'Or perhaps Byron. But Grand-mama ...'

'Were there *any* bedrooms at Denisthorn the dowager marchioness liked?' The question was put with a humorous smile. 'What was the little story?'

Geraldine paused to think. 'Do you know—you might be right!' She laughed too. 'It was difficult to find anything she liked, anywhere. Now, let me tell you what happened. It's some time ago now, a bit before either Athena or I were born. A bit before Papa and Mama were married.'

'A whole lifetime ago!'

'And since both my grandparents are no longer with us, I suppose the story can be relegated to Denisthorn myth and legend.'

They giggled together like schoolgirls.

'I am laughing with you without knowing the full story.'

'Well, listen to this, Sofia. And mind that I heard the story from a nanny, who told a companion, never from the protagonists themselves, or even my own parents. No one would talk about such incidents in polite conversation with a young unmarried girl, as I was when I heard it.'

Sofia's eyes widened. 'My goodness. Please, please do go on. The anticipation is unbearable.'

They walked together past the mirror lake in front of Denisthorn Hall, and Geraldine pointed out some significant landmarks from the height of the rise where the folly stood.

'Well, my grandfather, the fourth earl of Denisthorn, was a philanderer. In the days before my mother was mistress of the house, that is, before Grandpapa died, the rooms were named for the colour of their decoration, accessories, and accoutrements. I think it was the blue room then ... or the yellow room. Oh dear, I don't remember!'

'See? Legend and myth are full of forgotten details which are later embellished and embroidered to sound better than they were!'

They laughed together again, in the slight breeze that blew in from the direction of Gallantrae.

'So guests were staying in the rooms. And one afternoon, one of the lady guests had repaired to her room complaining of a headache. When Grand-mama knocked on her door after about an hour, to inquire after her, she discovered her in ... in what one might call a compromising situation with Grand-papa!'

'My goodness. I did suspect it might be something of that nature.'

'But that was not all.'

'Oh! It would have been enough to finish me, if I were the lady concerned ... *either* lady. Honestly—men!'

'Grand-mama was made of stern stuff. But she did discover him there again on another occasion, with *another* guest, who said he had taken advantage of her, which rumour had it she only said to protect her virtue.'

'Well, well—he was irrepressible.'

'What's more, he did it again, several months later, with a housemaid! A lot was made of her beauty and seductive powers. She could not have held her employ longer than that afternoon.'

'What—in that very room? He must have taken a liking it. Or he must have been quite ... ah remiss.'

'You mean *stupid*.' Geraldine laughed. 'I suppose it is all right to laugh now. Yes, my grandfather must have liked the room we now call Keats, because it has double doors. That is, two doors, opening in opposite directions, for quiet.'

'And for privacy, I would imagine.'

'Well, they did not work on those occasions.'

'Then there was the occasion when Grand-mama walked in without knocking.'

'What! Even if she knew what he was like?'

'*Because* she knew what he was like.'

'The story goes that she flounced in, flapping a fan, opening and shutting it like some Spanish dancer, and addressed the offenders where they lay. But she moved too close to the grate, and her skirts caught fire.'

'Are you sure you're not relating pages out of a novel?' Sofia laughed so hard she had to place a hand to her tightly-corseted waist.

'No—the stories came to me much as they happened. Well ... so I was told. And Grand-mama, from then on, was always sure to have a high fire-guard around her bedroom fires.'

'I suppose the more modern expedient of oil radiators would have prevented that accident.'

'Athena has radiators at Temple Grove. They are in the Russian ornate style, and cost a fortune to install. She has *two* in every single room.'

'So your sister has high ideals in style?'

'Her ambition in terms of style and comfort are without peer. And her husband indulges her. I have seen how he looks at her, with abject adoration.'

'So it's not only for money that she married.'

'She might have married for money, Athena was adamant about that ... after all Mr Phineas Gow is, if anything, increasing in wealth as we speak.'

Sofia took a quick inhalation of surprise.

'Yes,' Geraldine continued. 'She might have. But she does have Mr Gow's adulation. I do not know whether we should call it love.'

'Perhaps it is.'

'Does love not have to be returned to deserve that definition? I do not know at all how Athena feels.'

The breezeway at the stables at Denisthorn was a full illustration of its definition, Geraldine thought. She had taken a walk instead of a ride on the day Sofia left, to avoid riding alone, and to stave off exhaustion. She wandered down there with a steady stride and in a purposeful mood, hoping to meet Mary Mark. Wind tore at her skirts, and she clamped on to her hat and veil when she stopped at the entrance. Moving inward a few steps, she sought shelter in the lee of the stalls, then moved forward slowly.

She spied the girl, wearing tweed breeches and leather waistcoat and apron, surrounded by stableboys. Geraldine saw they were all rather young, the smallest among them perhaps not even twelve years of age. They listened earnestly to what the girl was saying, but she stopped as soon as she glimpsed her mistress at the end of the cobbled breezeway. She gave a cursory bow, knowing a bob or curtsey would appear rather strange in the clothes she wore. Tearing herself away from the knot of boys, she approached Geraldine.

'Good morning, my lady.'

'Is there somewhere we can have a word, Mark?'

They moved to a tack room, which Geraldine did not think to be absolutely appropriate, but she had to make allowances for haste and expediency.

'I have heard of your father's wishes for you, Mark.'

The girl hung her head. 'I knew I should not have said a word in the courtyard, then, my lady.'

'No—don't regret it.' She smiled to reassure her. 'I am here to ask you something.'

'I cannot continue here. Father wants me to ask Mrs Beste if I can work in the kitchen. Here or at Gallantrae. I cannot do that!' She blurted out the words then slapped fingers to mouth. 'I'm sorry. I'm so sorry, my lady. This is no business to address to you.'

Geraldine started another sentence.

But the girl continued. 'I shall run away. I cannot help myself. I'll wait for a dark night, but I cannot take one of your horses, my lady! I'll pack a bag and find some other stables somewhere. Every tavern has a stable.'

'A tavern is no place for the likes of you, Mary. Now listen. Take a breath and listen. I have a suggestion which I think your father might approve. Even though I strongly believe you should make your own decisions.'

Disbelief made a strong look of surprise on the girl's face. It was as if she listened to a fairy tale. She was working class and a woman. Most of the aspects of her life were determined by man or master. Or at the least by a mistress.

This was where Geraldine could step in, and she did. 'Cheltenham House is soon to be taken by Miss Bridwell, who is coming to live here permanently. She will need someone to take charge of the stables.'

'At Cheltenham House? There is but one set of stalls and the carriage horse used to be stabled at the tavern.'

'Changes are afoot. Everything will be done well, accommodating two mounts and a carriage horse. Would you be willing to take charge, and also pay attention to how the gardens are cared for?'

The girl's jaw dropped and she closed her mouth quickly, out of politeness. 'My father will only be persuaded if ...'

'I promise the salary will be generous.'

'Will I be a groom, then, my lady?'

'Mary,' Geraldine took a breath, knowing she was taking a risk that was by no means small. 'You will be coachman and second gardener. I think I can call the old second gardener back, in the absence of Cox, who has gone off to Windsor.'

'Yes, I heard he has.'

'Bellhouse still finds his way to that rose bower to prune it. I noticed last time I was there. He hid behind the greenhouse.' She smiled. 'Do you think you can do three horses, two stable boys, and deal with all that goes with renovating the stables?'

Mary Mark shifted on her feet. She seemed to be thinking fast.

'I don't want you to think only of leaving the bailiwick of your father, but also of managing and increasing your own skills.'

'I do not think a girl ...'

'How old are you now, Mary?'

'I'm nearly twenty, my lady.'

'A woman, then. And yes—a woman can do all a man can, and more, because we think differently, and we consider the welfare of both people and beasts.'

Again, the girl's eyes rounded with wonder.

'Do you think you have the skills? You will have help, as I enumerated. You can give me your response in a few days. But we cannot tarry with this.'

Mary Mark nodded, and bowed. And then a wide smile decorated her smudged face. 'I can do it, ma'am. I shall do it, my lady. My response is yes, yes, I can do it if you will give me the chance.'

'The chance is yours, Mary.' Geraldine turned, fought the stiff draught at the mouth of the breezeway, and made her way back to the house. She had forgotten to tell Mary Mark to keep the news to herself, remembering the ironic remark that there were *no secrets at Denisthorn Hall*.

Just before she got to the edge of the mirror lake, where the dome of the distant folly seemed to be hidden in a mist, she heard the pounding of running steps behind her, and turned. The wind nearly whipped her hat off her head.

'Mary Mark!'

'My lady. My lady, I'm here to say sorry.'

Disappointment made Geraldine's shoulders droop, but she valiantly held on to her hat. 'Oh no, Mary.'

'I'm sorry I was so discourteous when you went riding with your companion. Miss ... Miss ...'

'Miss Bridwell. Well, I forgive you heartily, Mary, for I do not even remember you being remiss.' She laughed. 'Are you still happy to take the position at Cheltenham House?'

'More than happy, my lady. May I say something else?'

Geraldine nodded.

'I was angry because I wanted to be out riding with you myself.' She hung her head, as was her way.

'Oh, Mark, you goose. There will be other occasions. It will not cease entirely. I shall ride out with you in borrowed clothes again, and we shall shock the birds by riding astride. Off with you. And please expect a message for you to come up to the house soon.' She turned and walked on. After a few paces, she turned. 'And Mary—leave it to me to tell your father. It will work better coming from me. Goodbye now.'

'Goodbye, my lady. And thank you.'

The letter that arrived from Sofia Bridwell in the second post dampened the good mood upon which Geraldine had sailed in on, after the windy walk, and sat down to luncheon. She simply removed hat and veil in her room, without bothering to summon Fairley, and went down as she was.

The letter was long, and it startled her, even if it confirmed some of her suspicions. Sofia described her father's opposition to her taking up Cheltenham House on her own.

> *My father is totally opposed to my plans. He said he is fully dismayed, and my rejection of Sir Anthony is 'without reason'. But it is true that he cannot stop me. And neither can he place impediments to my using my own fortune as I see fit. His hands are tied, and my way is free to take, but I cannot do it without placing a big burden on our relationship as father and daughter. He will not be willing to continue as we are, and will come close to severing our connection. To think we were so close when I was a little girl!*
>
> *I think if Mother were still with us, she would take his side, stating it was her duty to*

oppose my plans.

In addition, dear Geraldine, he says my lady's maid is in his employ, not mine, so she will not be allowed to move with me. Neither will I be allowed any horses. So I shall lose my beloved, beloved Gunner. He will be lost to me. I have had him since I turned thirteen.

I have been in a lather all day, retiring to my room with a headache.

But I emerged determined and purposeful, because the dream of being in charge of my own destiny is too strong and too tempting to allow anything to get in the way. I shall come, I shall take Cheltenham House, but I should have to seek a lady's maid. I should also need to seek another banker; one less subject to my father's influence. It will be no small undertaking, in addition to the move, but it will have to be done.

Geraldine admired Sofia's willingness to sever ties, because it also meant social isolation in a sense, from those who thought along the same lines as her father and Sir Anthony Ross. There would be something of a scandal. She was sure Sofia knew it—they had discussed it enough—and was willing to risk it.

She pulled the bell. 'Please tell Prudhomme I should like a word in the small sitting room.'

'*Prudhomme*, my lady?'

'You heard, Formby.'

Her mother's maid stood on Geraldine's sitting room carpet in less than five minutes.

'Prudhomme—I won't keep you long. Do you remember Mary Burgess?'

'She was the dowager marchioness's maid, my lady.'

'Do we know her whereabouts?'

'No, but I shall enquire, if that is what you wish.'

'Please do. I do hope she is willing to consider a position.' Geraldine could tell from the prudent and discreet maid's face that her maturity and experience did not allow her to ask any questions. 'Your position, Prudhomme, is not in question, and neither is Fairley's position. Nothing will change at Denisthorn. I would appreciate it if you were discreet.'

'Very discreet, your ladyship.' She bobbed and left, pulling the door behind her.

She had hardly left when Formby was in again, announcing a visitor. 'Sir Bernard Bridwell, my lady.'

Geraldine felt faint. She was not fully prepared to face an unexpected visit from Sofia's father.

Lady Athena Gow looked mature and handsome in dark blue embroidered muslin, which was obviously expensively done for her in India. The tiniest of lace caps was attached to her elaborately-styled hair. A pair of sapphire earrings Geraldine had never seen her wear before twinkled in the sunlight.

The sisters embraced, and moved off the forecourt at Temple Grove.

'I am so happy to have you here, Geraldine.'

'Only one or two days, because Cousin Angus arrives from Edinburgh on Friday.'

Athena whirled around like a Turkish dervish. '*Geraldine!*'

Her sister stared, uncomprehending. 'What is it, Athena?'

'You called him Cousin Angus.'

Geraldine held fingers to lips.

'He is your husband. You ... we ... I ... ah. I see what the problem is.'

'I didn't know there was a problem.'

Athena took her sister's arm and fairly pulled her through the well-appointed hall, past a bank of closed doors to a sumptuous sitting room, whose fittings and furniture still emitted a new smell, where the sting of polish was still in the air, and where a small Pekingese puppy sat on a cushion. She scooped the dog up while still grasping Geraldine's elbow. 'Meet Augustine.'

Geraldine was speechless, both at her verbal transgression and at the sight of her sister's pet.

'I call him Gus.'

'Are you serious?'

'Very—he is a gift from Phineas, who begins to know me very, very well.' She simpered and tilted her head, then dropped a kiss on the puppy's nose. It hardly moved.

Geraldine saw that a covered trolley waited in a corner.

'Connie will be in, in a minute, to pour us a cup, and you can refresh yourself. Because I do see ...' She looked sideways at her sister's eyes. 'Yes, Geraldine, there is. There is a problem. Sit down, take my hand, loosen your hat ribbons, and tell me.'

'You sound like Grand-mama used to.'

Athena ignored the remark, and continued, lowering her voice an octave. 'Have you and Angus um … is your marriage consummated, Geraldine?'

ooo

Here ends Book Two in the Denisthorn Hall Series.
To read more about the marriages of Lady Geraldine and
Lady Athena, the slow recovery of Lord Croukerne, the
decline of his wife Lady Edwina, more of the exploits of
Angus Crownrigg, and the arrival of Miss Sofia Bridwell
at Cheltenham House, be sure not to miss Book Three.
Click 'follow' on the Amazon book page for updates on
the author's publications. You will be notified of the next
release.